Comfort for Community

Heather Osoy

Copyright © 2023 by Heather Osoy
All rights reserved.
This is a work of fiction. Unless otherwise indicated, all the names, characters, places, events, and incidents in this book are either a product of the author's imagination or used in a fictitious manner. Any resemblance to actual events, places, or persons- living or dead- is coincidental.

Content Warning

This novel contains scenes of domestic abuse, attempted SA, abortion, some violence & racism.

Prologue

"Everyone loves smoothies."

The acting career of Theo Evans spanned a few decades. At twelve years old, his breakout role was in a sitcom that lasted several seasons. He then starred in a long list of box office hits that ranged from family-friendly to action-packed. While Evans never received an award for his work, he also didn't have a single scandal to his name. When he officially announced that he was running for president of the United States, most people approved. In fact, people from other countries wanted to see him win.

The charming, physically fit brunette bachelor in his early forties represented the change most people in the United States wanted to see. They wanted a shakeup within their government. Evans wasn't a career politician, he didn't have a running mate, and he didn't claim allegiance to any political party. He didn't need a party to stand behind him, and he proudly funded the campaign himself. As a result, there were no wealthy donors or corporations to satisfy. He sought validation from the general American public that already adored him.

Despite his wealth and overly handsome appearance, Evans was seen as relatable. His image generated nostalgia and joy. He wasn't boastful. During interviews, he said little, but smiled plenty. He rode the subway, dressed modestly, and didn't have a social media presence until his campaign.

His slogan was: "Simplicity." - making a point to include the period. Evans believed every American citizen deserved food, housing, and medical care outright. He believed that when everyone's basic emotional and physical needs were met, it would reduce desperation. Less desperation would result in less crime and a greater quality of life.

Merchandise spread like wildfire. Everyone wanted a basic black cap or shirt that read "Simplicity." on the front- especially social media influencers. There were hashtags, dance videos, videos showing off how much merchandise they had, and fan accounts. The momentum grew large in a short amount of time, and the concept of Simplicity was synonymous with Evans. As a result, the media branded supporters as Simples.

Rather than interpret the label as a sneaky insult, it was welcomed as a badge of pride. Simples connected online and at speaker events. Businesses took advantage of the interest by showing Evans's old movies in theaters, naming cocktails and sandwiches after him, offering discounts to people wearing merchandise, and doing anything else they could do to associate themselves with the popular candidate.

To no one's surprise, Evans won by a historic landslide- becoming the 54th president of the United States. Even with the campaign over, Simples continued to display flags, posters, and other memorabilia on their cars and homes. They continued to wear "Simplicity." hats, shirts, and sweatshirts. Social media was instrumental in the continued growth of Simples, and Evans curiously didn't cease his speaking events around the country.

Politicians eager to align themselves with Evans formed the Simply American party. They did so in hopes that the growing support base would stand behind their own political ambitions. Due to there not being an appointed Vice President, the Speaker of the House of Representatives- a newly identified Simple- quietly served the role. Some major corporations, concerned about their bottom line, also looked to Simples. They sponsored Evans's speaking events and donated to the Simply American party. Although Evans initially made a point not to be a member of any party, he didn't disagree with the creation of an organization based on his own ideology. He also didn't see the hypocrisy in his acceptance of corporate donations. Moreover, the same Simples who were impressed by Evans's independence from big businesses and career politicians during his campaign didn't protest his conflicting behavior after winning the election.

Abortion had already been banned for the second time. While Evans claimed to support a woman's right to choose, he saw reproduction as a concern for the Greater Good. For decades, the country's marriage and childbirth rates were dramatically low due to a high cost of living and low wages. After increasing the minimum wage to $30 per hour, and reworking the nation's budget to provide affordable housing and free public education through a bachelor's degree, the president was confident more people would build families.

Same-sex couples were lured with financial incentives to adopt children. What stood out to members of the LGBTQ+ community about the forms, however, was the language. Applicants specifically had to be married and monogamous, and they were only given the choice to identify themselves as either *he* or *she*. When opponents addressed the president about their concerns, Evans redirected them to his campaign slogan.

He insisted on the following: "Children need stability. As individuals, we are free to live as we want. When one settles down to start a family, there are other people to consider. It doesn't make sense to complicate things. I know people are different, and being different isn't bad or wrong. Creating excessive differences, however, takes us further away from Simplicity. It creates conflict. It builds walls. I don't want walls between us. Now, I know change is hard. We've been raised to accept all differences, but it's also in our nature to evolve. Through common ground... Simplicity.... our American children will thrive."

Evans didn't stop there. He labeled ethnicity as equally complicated. Nationality was useful, because he celebrated all Americans. He prized citizenship, because he valued all who wanted to be American. Ethnicity, according to Evans, brought attention to *ancestors'* nationality and citizenship. He claimed that it distanced people from their current American identity. For the sake of Simplicity, he signed an executive order that people nicknamed the "Don't Say Ethnicity" law. Evans stressed the importance of people remembering their ancestors' positive personality traits, and direct contributions to American culture. He warned that a focus on ethnicity watered those contributions down.

Concern was growing about the president's ideology. Opponents argued that America was never homogenous. Censoring their families' histories not only felt disrespectful; it felt like a denial of what made them unique. People worried that the president ultimately wanted to downplay the many hardships people faced and continued to face on American soil because of those differences. No longer legitimizing those hardships could result in the erasure of relevant and protective policies.

Evans reminded his critics about his campaign promise, and his responsibility to fulfill that promise to those who voted for him. He repeated that he didn't see differences as bad, but he thought they brought unnecessary complications. He claimed to want what was best for the country, and knew his methods would be met with resistance by some. He issued a compromise, saying that people were free to identify with whichever ethnicity they chose, but it would not be recognized by law, and public declaration would be considered a disturbance of the peace. While Simples applauded Evans's flexibility, others complained that their concerns were glossed over, and he was just rephrasing himself.

To no one's surprise, Evans ran for a second term. Only, not everyone was on board like before. Simples took it upon themselves to drown out the opposition. They were blinded by their affection for Evans as an entertainer, the thriving economy his policies created, and the strong familial connection they felt with other Simples. While mental health services were made widely accessible, most Simples insisted that they didn't need it- so long as they had each other. They, as well as members of the Simply American Party and contributing donors, didn't see the community sustaining without their founding father in a position of power.

They intimidated neighbors, co-workers and family members. Fan groups created social media events that involved parading through cities with signs and flags. They stole mail-in ballots, and arrived at polling places to force their opinions on those in line. If their words didn't intimidate enough, their arsenal did. When all was said and done, Evans won a second term by a small margin. Once sworn in, he didn't waste a single moment.

He gave family physicians the responsibility of declaring babies' races upon birth. They were provided with the options: red, brown, black, white and yellow. Parents weren't allowed input, and their offspring were never allowed to disagree with their own coding. As a result, children's races reflected more of what their physicians assumed, than of their parents' actual backgrounds. Evans insisted that color coding was the way to go, and minimizing discussion added to its simplicity.

Naturally, interracial marriage became the next target. The president argued that mixing races created the burden of families feeling less like a cohesive unit.

"For example," he said. "What if you have a white father, a yellow mother, and a brown child? How do you think that child is going to feel? What quality of life do you think that child will have? How connected will that child feel to his or her own family? Without connection, there will be desperation, and that desperation will sour America in that child's eyes. For the sake of our nation's strength, we must keep life simple. I'm keeping my end of the bargain. Love who you want, but when it comes to breeding future Americans, we must be responsible."

In addition, Evans referred to those of mixed race and in interracial relationships as the Blended- comparing them to smoothies.

"Everyone loves smoothies. They taste great, and provide us with lots of nutrients. The drawback is you don't always know what you're getting. There could be something you're allergic to. How fresh was the fruit? Was anything added to change the color or taste? Some kind of powder or syrup? You think that smoothie is good for you. Everyone says it is, but is it really? When you have a pure piece of fruit, you know what you're getting. You can see the freshness, and know where the flavor came from. Nothing else was added, and it is good for you. To mix is to create uncertainty. Purity is simple."

He gave the nation a six-month warning. Interracial couples had to nullify their unions, and find separate living arrangements. Their children needed to receive color-coding reassignments, then reside with family members of the same color code. If no immediate family members shared the same color code, then the children had to be surrendered to the state. The six-month warning also affected transracial adoption. The influx of same-sex couples drawn in to adopt just a couple of years prior were suddenly at risk of losing the children they took in. Single adults, as well as any older children and teens without a color code, were given a year to be assigned one. Those not in compliance risked arrest.

Evans then encouraged his supporters to end any discussion of race in a negative manner. When opponents raised their eyebrows and cited the First Amendment of the U.S. Constitution, Evans cited Brandenburg v. Ohio. He assured them that preventing hateful language towards a race was a good thing, and he wanted to encourage unifying discussion when it came to differences. With the entire Supreme Court rolling over in the president's favor, criticisms in terms of race could no longer be written, printed, posted or spoken legally.

During one of his many speaking events, Evans told the crowd, "They say: if you don't learn from the past, you are doomed to repeat it. I disagree. We have learned. That's why we're better than we ever have been. Many atrocities occurred in this country on behalf of race, and that's the point. It's all past tense. We're not learning when we dwell. We lack pride when all we hear about it is what we've done wrong. That mentality is unhealthy, and only promoted by those who want to live in fear. They want legislation that gives special accommodation to groups they want you to believe are marginalized. To receive any level of accommodation is a sign of privilege. So how unfortunate are they really? My presidency has resulted in record-low incarceration rates. The average American isn't struggling financially. We have roofs over our heads, and ample food in our bellies. Our quality of life has dramatically improved. Why? We learned from our mistakes. Oppression doesn't exist, so there's no need to behave as if it does."

Protesters immediately took to the streets. One of the many things they pointed out was how Evans threatened any defiance with prison time. They questioned how low the incarceration rate really was- given all the new restrictions. While many prisons had been dismantled, and the overall prison population was at a record low, the nation's crime rate was higher than ever. Activists blamed Simples, and the authorities' willingness to keep records of their harassment and violence, but not make them accountable.

While there was no more widespread hunger and homelessness, people outside of the Simple circle lived in fear. Many turned to mental health services, but with Evans' influence firmly in place, there wasn't much room to heal. Anxiety was especially high among the Blended. Many couples continued to see each other in secret, and children were hidden in their homes.

Those who remained out in the open spearheaded what became known as the #goback Movement. It encouraged non-white Americans to flee to the countries of their ancestors- the same ancestors they weren't allowed to acknowledge through ethnicity. The movement was sold as a compassionate alternative to staying and fighting, because it provided Blended people with *their own* Simplicity. Evans approved to such an extent, he allowed the loudest Blended supporters leniency. Officially, they were newly referred to as Go-To's. The general public, on the other hand, called them Twos- as they were known to be branded with the number two somewhere on the body. While Simples thought of Twos as humanitarians, they were more so seen by the Blended as international traffickers and sellout informants for the Simply American Party.

The governor of West Texas soon introduced his own solution: the Comfort for Community law. It enabled the Blended to remain in the country by vowing not to arrest those who turn themselves in, and provided urgency to pregnant women. Details were unclear, as its secrecy granted full protection for those who utilized the law, but it was well understood that Evans didn't endorse it. For many, that was reason enough to trust it. Gradually, several other states initiated their own versions of Comfort for Community.

1

"You aren't supposed to be here."

Morning sickness causes a lapse in judgment, resulting in the accidental burning of her husband's scrambled eggs. A rush of panic blankets Gertrude's nausea as her husband stands up from the table, then slaps her as hard as he can. No words come out of his mouth, and he hardly looks her in the eye. While he quietly finishes the bacon and pancakes on his plate, Gertrude is left sobbing on the floor.

Richard, her husband, is 11 years her senior, and a long-time friend of her father. To ensure that Gertrude - an only child- would marry a man worthy of her father's approval, she was promised to the family friend back when she was a preteen. The pair also happens to have the same bright blonde hair and ocean blue eyes.

***

Many parents were concerned about their kids risking arrest by venturing romantically outside of their color code. As a precaution, most kids were forbidden to befriend anyone whose skin didn't closely resemble theirs. Parents put pressure on politicians, who- in turn- put pressure on public school districts to segregate by withholding funding. Meanwhile, segregated learning pods grew in popularity.

Gertrude grew up attending one herself. Pods ensured that children not only grew up around those of the same color code, but also of the same economic class. To fit Evans's standards on race and ethnicity when it came to history, only the contemporary period was taught, and lessons were framed in the perspective of the learning pod's color code. There was no need to racially diversify the curriculum, as all Americans were encouraged to believe they had the same origin and experiences.

Married girls were allowed to drop out of school, as their unions promoted family development. Family development was deemed a higher priority for girls than their education. Gertrude was allowed to finish high school, but was married off as soon as she did.

She smiled and obeyed- despite hardly knowing the man chosen to be her husband. Richard behaved more like an extension of her father, but he was far less loving. He was condescending, demanding and cold. He instructed Gertrude how to dress and behave herself in his presence. She wasn't allowed to rest. There was always something to clean or organize, or fix about herself. When Gertrude somehow didn't meet her husband's high expectations, she was berated and beaten.

Richard blamed his actions on his responsibility to the nation. He was as avid a Simple as her parents- wanting nothing less than what Evans promoted. He believed that providing his wife with a strict routine eliminated all wiggle room for outlets and social circles that promoted recklessness. By focusing on Richard and the home, Gertrude was fulfilling her duties as a Simple wife.

It didn't take long for Gertrude to fulfill another duty: becoming pregnant with one of the many children Richard intended to have. Although the 18 year-old received much praise for her quiet, smiling performance as a devoted wife, she was deeply unhappy. At 7 weeks pregnant, she already had a plan brewing for her escape.

***

Richard continues to ignore her as he gets up and walks out of the house. As soon as Gertrude hears his car leave the driveway, she springs into action.

At the nearby department store, she buys dark brown hair dye, and foundation that is a few shades darker than her beige skin tone. When she returns home, she packs a small suitcase, and then gets started on her hair. Once her hair is dyed, dried and styled in her usual updo, she applies the foundation to her face, neck and ears. To cover the rest of her skin, she wears a long-sleeved shirt and an ankle-length overall dress. Gertrude opts for gardening gloves on her hands, as she fears any makeup on them will smear. Since it's early summer, she doesn't think the gloves will look too out of place.

When she closes and locks the front door for the final time, she takes a deep breath. She tries her best to brush away her growing sense of shame as she walks back to the car, throws the suitcase on the front passenger's seat, then drives to the police station.

Parked in the lot, she attempts to calm her nerves. She asks herself if she is sure about what she's planning to do, because the idea of stepping out of the car terrifies her. There aren't many steps to take from her car to the entrance of the police station, but there are many risks. Blended children were reassigned and relocated after the implementation of the color code system, but the racially ambiguous-looking adults they inevitably became are seen as abominations. Simples have a history of violence towards anyone they assume is Blended, and most people look the other way.

After finally building up the courage to step out of her car with the suitcase, Gertrude moves as quickly as she can. She bursts through the swinging glass doors with such abrupt force, she catches everyone's attention. She can feel her body want to retreat, so she uses all the energy she can muster to push herself forward. As her body moves closer and closer to the front desk, her eyes stick to the floor.

"Excuse me," she tells the officer at the counter. He's an older, pale-skinned man with freckles and a lush head of gray hair.

All eyes are on her. Those who aren't wide-eyed and slack-jawed express disgust. Gertrude can feel her heart pounding inside of her chest, as she raises her glance to meet the officer's.

"I'm not sure who I need to speak to. I'm here to turn myself in."

The officer narrows his gaze. "Are you... Blended?"

"Yes...and I'm pregnant."

There is an audible gasp. Gertrude keeps her eyes on the officer, too afraid to see how others are viewing her.

"Thank you for fulfilling your responsibility," says the officer with a sigh. "A nurse will be with you shortly."

At that very instant, a middle-aged nurse in lavender scrubs steps out with a clipboard. She has almond skin, and moisturized braids pulled back into a half ponytail. Her smile is warm and wide.

"Good morning, Miss. I'll be taking care of you today. Please follow me."

Gertrude is guided into a medical examination room. The nurse's smile never leaves her face, as she warns that any refusal of care will result in arrest. Gertrude is then instructed to take off her ballet flats. She only put makeup on the visible skin of her feet, hoping to mimic a bad tan. Thankfully, the nurse doesn't appear suspicious, and she has no interest in the teen fully disrobing.

Gertrude's picture is taken. She's made to step on a scale for her weight and height, then the nurse checks her blood pressure. Afterward, she's told to urinate in a cup in an adjacent bathroom. Once completed, she's injected with a mysterious substance in the back of her neck. No small talk is made, and Gertrude is too afraid to ask questions.

"So far, so good," beams the nurse. "You're indeed pregnant. I just need to ask you a few questions before we conclude."

"Um…Okay."

"Date of birth?"

"June 11th, 2054."

"Birthplace?"

"Here in West Texas."

The nurse slightly cocks her head to the side and pauses. "Hmm. Did you know this was the first state to implement the Comfort program? Back in '63? You were…" She checks the clipboard. "…Born in '54. So, that would make you… 9 years-old then. Been out and about all this time. Interesting you're turning yourself in *now*."

A sudden wave of warmth passes through Gertrude's body, and her mind swirls. She didn't think she'd be met with any sort of judgment by the people running the program. Unable to think of a better way to respond, she shrugs her shoulders.

The nurse continues. "What are your father and mother's color codes?"

"Um… they're both white." Gertrude looks down, as she's able to come up with a lie. "I was adopted as a baby, and never surrendered to the state. I always knew I looked different from my parents, but they never talked about codes or the Comfort law. I

18

don't know why. I only learned about all that stuff recently. I came here, because I want to do the right thing."

The nurse gives a reassuring smile. She makes a few notes, then points to the teen's belly. "What is the expectant father's color code?"

"White, and he's my husband."

"Okay. I'm going to need you to provide your husband's name, your home address, and where your husband works. I also need information on your parents' whereabouts. I have those spaces highlighted on this form here. It is standard that you, a surrendered Blended, chart that information by your own hand."

The nurse hands over her clipboard with a pen. Gertrude momentarily reconsiders what she's about to do, but there's no room for choice at that point. Once she finishes writing down the needed information, she returns the items back to the nurse.

Scanning the information with her eyes, the nurse grins, "Perfect. So, how much do you know about the Comfort for Community Law?"

"I knew enough to come here. That's all, really."

The nurse's tone continues to be uncomfortably cheerful. "Well, Miss. You aren't supposed to be here. Your creation and birth went against President Evan's plan for the nation, and your adoptive parents raised you without authorization. For that, they will be arrested. Your husband will be arrested for his knowledge of your existence, and his decision to unionize and breed with you. Your child can not be born, and you are not allowed to return to your address. For your safety, I will provide you with a re-classification. Then, the state will provide you with a new name and family. Your previous life does not exist. If it is discovered that you speak of or interact with your old life in any form, your protection will be forfeited, and you will be arrested for treason. It is also illegal to speak, write or post about your experience with Comfort for Community. Any questions before we proceed?"

Gertrude is unaware that she is holding her breath and clenching her teeth. She feels overwhelming guilt, and tears begin to form in her eyes.

After a little bit of hesitation, she asks, "Will the new family know about me being Blended?"

"They will know of the information we provide. Any knowledge of your past life will implicate them."

Gertrude looks at the floor. "And if I run into my parents or husband?"

"You have no husband, and you haven't met your parents yet. Any others you're alluding to… Don't worry about running into them. You never will."

The nurse proceeds to speak while looking down and making notes on her clipboard. "I'm going to provide you with abortion pills. You're 18, but you can pass for younger. You are now 16. Based on your blue eyes, and relatively light brown skin, I'm going to code you as white. Bleaching cream and hair dye will be mailed immediately to your new residence. The hair dye is optional. The abortion pills and bleaching cream are not. All are provided free of charge by the state…your new state of residence, I mean. You will be flown to the state of North California. Now, before I go, I will provide you with some maxi pads."

She takes a box from the cupboard, and hands it over rather hurriedly.

"Put one on as soon as I leave, then put the rest in your suitcase. An officer will arrive within a few minutes to provide you with transportation to the airport. At this very moment, they are preparing your new identification card. Thank you for your service, and for providing a Simple comfort to the community. Best of luck to you."

The nurse leaves the examination room, closing the door behind her. Gertrude puts her shoes back on. Sitting in silence, she realizes that she's facing a frightening, uncertain future alone. She wipes away the moisture from her eyes.

Suddenly, the door bursts open. It's an officer wearing head-to-toe tactical gear. Gertrude is unsure of what he's protecting himself from, and wonders why she isn't receiving the same level of protection. She's also bothered by her inability to read the officer's facial expressions- due to his balaclava mask, ballistic helmet, and dark sunglasses. Although the nurse's smile came across as disingenuous, she somehow appeared more human than the officer currently is.

The officer holds out a white pill and a small plastic cup of water.

"Hold the pill under your tongue until completely dissolved, then drink."

Gertrude does as she's told. Then, the officer hands her a small box of more pills.

"Keep with you, or else."

An index card is handed to her. Written in ink is her color code as white, her age as 16, her flight information, and her new name: Dinah Clark.

"Keep that card with you," says the officer. "They will provide you with an official identification card as soon as you land in North California. Until then, the loss of that card will be considered forfeiture of protection, and you will be arrested for treason. Understand?"

Dinah nods. She places the pills and index card inside one of her large side pockets. The officer then escorts her to the back of the building- where there's an unmarked sedan with tinted windows waiting. In the driver's seat is a casually dressed man with dark hair, and warm yellow undertone skin. He doesn't say one word, or look anywhere else other than what is directly in front of him. The officer sits next to him in the front passenger seat, while Dinah sits in the back with her suitcase.

The officer turns his head to face her. "Those pills. Take them out now."

Dinah does as she's told.

"Now listen to me very carefully: put two pills between your cheek and gum. Put the other two between your other cheek and gum. Let them sit and dissolve. Do nothing else until I tell you."

Dinah opens the box, pushes the pills out of their foil packaging, then places them where they need to go. As soon as she completes her task, the car takes off. She has never been to the airport- much less on a plane, so she's very nervous. The quiet car ride makes it easier for her anxiety to swell. When they finally pull up to the airport, she's instructed by the officer to enter on her own, and to follow the flight itinerary exactly.

After checking in, handing over her suitcase, and passing through security, Dinah rushes to the women's restroom. She somehow managed to forget about her fading makeup, but that's not what catches her off guard when she takes her gardening gloves off to wash her hands. Dinah's skin tone is noticeably lighter than her natural hue. Taking advantage of being the only one in the restroom, she rinses off what she can of her foundation, then dries herself with paper towels. The sight of her bright skin instantly releases tension from the teen's shoulders.

During the flight, Dinah experiences horrible cramps and a mild headache. She's thankful for the maxi pads, because she's also bleeding. She knows she's losing the baby. She wants to cry, but tries her best to hold it together. She's sure someone is monitoring her behavior on the plane.

As soon as she arrives in North California, a tawny-skinned man in sweats approaches her with a card and then scurries away. It's her new identification card. The photo is what the nurse took at the police station, and it was altered to make Dinah's skin look as light as it happened to look at that moment.

Just then, a feminine voice calls out, "Dinah!"

The teen looks around. She meets eyes with a white, middle-aged couple that looks ecstatic to see her. Their brown hair and eyes remind Dinah of her birth parents. In all the chaos, she almost forgot about them. The woman approaches for a hug. Dinah is caught off guard by the familiarity and affection.

It is relieving for her to know that thinking for herself isn't so reckless after all. She sees herself as capable and in control for the first time. She also likes herself better as a brunette.

2

"No use for idle hands, and we want you to be visible."

"So glad you made it safely."

The woman is smiling wide at me. Her thin, unbuttoned sweater drapes over her ankle-length denim dress. Just like every other woman I've ever known, there's no proof of curvature at all. Her long, brunette hair is styled in a standard half ponytail. Besides her round-rimmed glasses, nothing about her look stands out. She might as well be my mom.

She turns to her husband. "Isn't she beautiful?" He gives an awkward smile and nods.

I look around. I don't know what I was expecting. I've never been outside of my neighborhood, let alone another state. Everyone looks like a variation of my parents. The women are wearing their long hair down, while the girls are wearing their hair up, and all of the boys and men have the same side part. Dresses and pants, purses and belts, and everyone has the same exhausted smile.

The woman gives me another hug. This time, it lingers. I always wanted my mom to hug me, so I should appreciate this. Instead, this feels like judgment. I'm cheating. I don't want to think about what might be happening to my mom right now. I can't save her. I can't undo all of this. Part of me misses her, though. I'm not sure why.

I catch myself. I can't let my mind wander too much. I don't want the woman to sense anything is off. I am present. I am grateful. I hold her as tightly as she holds me.

"I'm so glad you're here," the woman whispers into my ear, as she finally lets go of me.

The man clears his throat. "Welcome to the Clark family, Dinah. I'm Jaxtyn, and this is my wife, Quinn. We're very happy to have you here with us."

I try my best not to stare at his brunette hairpiece. I find it interesting that women aren't allowed to be vain, and we must follow the alleged laws of nature. Meanwhile, this guy can pretend that hair is still growing from his scalp. I force a smile back, but I make sure not to smile too big. I can't risk taking up too much space- even with my facial muscles.

The man is awkward like my dad. At least, he's smiling. My dad was very dedicated to his roles as financial provider and rule enforcer. I only heard from him when I did something wrong, then he sent me off to marry a man who was the same way. Hearing this new guy say he's happy to have me feels like some sort of humility test. I respond by keeping my mouth shut, looking down, and forming the tiniest smile possible.

The woman takes me by the hand. Both she and her husband continue smiling as we walk to their station wagon. I can't push my guard down. I'm certain that I'm being lured into some kind of trap. Any moment, their expressions will change, then they'll let me know how they really feel. Maybe we're not really going back to their house. Maybe they already found a husband for me. I did all of this just to land right back where I was.

The drive is quiet. I try to look as if my mind isn't all over the place. Maybe that's the game. Maybe I need to be laid back and pleasant on top of being meek. I have to seem approachable. At the same time, I can't initiate conversation or seem too excited. It's driving me crazy not knowing exactly what they need from me. I look to Quinne woman for clues. She knows what's expected of her. As soon as she sees me looking at her through the side mirror, she just smiles. What am I supposed to do with that? I guess I'll just smile back.

The man's voice interrupts my thoughts. "Put your head down."

I do as I'm told. "Yes, Sir."

That can only mean we're driving through areas I'm not allowed to be in. I close my eyes. I'm realizing how tired I am. It's been a long day. I can't sleep just yet, though, so I open my eyes and take a deep breath. Without looking up, I can see trees on both sides of us. Moments later, we're in the same kind of residential area I grew up in.

"Head up."

"Yes, Sir."

We approach the driveway of a beige two-story house with a large Simple flag mounted to it. It looks no different than the house my husband owned, and the one that my father owned. The sight of it makes me feel a bit dizzy. The woman opens the car door for me, then extends her hand to lead me out. I don't want to move, but that's not my choice to make. Both of them are still smiling... silently. My face hurts from smiling back at them.

As I walk towards the front door, the woman has her hand on my back. The feeling of her touch is becoming a little repulsive. She does it too much, but I can't push her away. They could turn me away, though. I'm not really their daughter, yet somehow the man still owns me. I'm an investment. If I can't prove my worth to the Greater Good, I'm worthless to them. I'm so angry with myself. I'm not better off than I was this morning.

The man opens the door. "Welcome home, Dinah."

The woman cheers. I mimic her, but I still feel uneasy. I have to push myself to walk inside the house. Suddenly, I'm right back in my old world. Not every Simple household has a flag posted outside, but all of them look exactly the same inside. There are various shades of white and beige, but no variation in texture or pattern. There's no decor of any kind, no houseplants, and no pictures. Bedrooms have the same bedspread and minimal furniture. The only ounce of personality one can find in any Simple home is based on gender roles. Bathrooms are full of feminine hygiene and cosmetic products, while garages are full of tools and sporting equipment. Pattern and color variation can be found on clothing. Other than that, there's nothing else to stress individualism, or importance in anything beyond the Greater Good. Even tending to pets is seen as fulfilling a duty, because they do their part in serving Simples.

The woman takes me to my colorless bedroom upstairs. It has a twin bed, a window without blinds, and a closet.

"Welcome to your very own room. I'll have you enrolled in a proper learning pod in time for Fall. Meanwhile, there's plenty of time to settle in."

"Thank you, Ma'am." I decide to pick her brain a little. "I'm close to finishing my studies too, Ma'am."

The woman laughs. "Your father sees a different goal. We want you to be comfortable with us and the neighborhood, and we want to find the right match for you. That's going to take time. School will allow you to spend that time productively. No use for idle hands, and we want you to be visible. If we play our cards right, you'll be married soon anyway."

I feel as if I've been punched in the gut. Hope is pointless, and- of course- this place is temporary. What have I gotten myself into?

"Poor thing." The woman's frown is exaggerated. "You've lost so much already. Your father and I are here to keep you on the righteous and Simple path."

"Thank you, Ma'am." I wonder what she means by that. How much does she know? Am I allowed to ask her? I really need to sit down.

The woman picks up on my growing anxiety. With her stuck-on friendly face, she asks, "What's on your mind?"

"May I... um... ask what they told you about me, Ma'am?"

"You sure you want to talk about that right now?"

"Yes, Ma'am. I mean..." I need to come up with an excuse quickly. Maybe knowing what she knows will help me think of a way to get out of here. I can't stay here. "... I guess I'm a little embarrassed."

"Embarrassed? I don't see how. The adoption agency told us you were raised in a proper, Simple home. That home caught fire, and you were the only survivor. Dinah, that broke our hearts. We wanted to give you a good home right away. We'll never be able to make up for what you've lost, but we're here for you now. We'll do our absolute best for you, because that's what we do. We look out for each other."

She reminds me so much of my mom, but I don't want to think about that right now. "Thank you, Ma'am."

"Of course. Anything else?"

I shake my head.

"Oh, and I almost forgot..."

The woman rushes out of my bedroom so quickly, I almost think to follow her. Instead, I stay put. A couple of minutes later, she brings back a medium-sized cardboard box with *Dinah* written on it with a black permanent marker. She puts it on the bed. A box cutter sits on top.

"This is for you. It's some kind of care package from the agency."

She takes the box cutter, and cuts through the tape on the top. "There. We've already been told by the agency to not poke our noses in. I'll see myself out."

"Thank you, Ma'am."

The woman leaves and actually closes the door behind her. That throws me off. Being allowed such privacy would be nice, but I'm sure this is a test. I'm going to open this box now, and be careful of my reaction. Either that woman is standing right outside the door, or maybe there are cameras. The man has been very quiet. He might have been watching and listening this entire time. I've heard of some Simple parents installing cameras all over their homes. I don't think my parents ever did that, but I'm sure my husband did.

I open the box. I pull the layer of filler paper out and throw it on the floor. I gasp. The package is full of boxed blonde hair dye, and 30ml wide-mouth jars of Enlightenment- a skin-bleaching cream. A letter sits on top. It reads:

Hello, Dinah

You are being supplied with menstrual pads, cosmetic products, and instructions. Expect refills to be mailed to you on a monthly basis. Each package is funded by the state of North California, on behalf of the Comfort for Community Program. It is against the law for you to refuse what you are being provided. In addition, any proven discussion, display or sale of the contents within this and all upcoming packages will nullify your agreement and lead to your arrest. Thank you for your willful participation in the Comfort for Community Program. Enjoy your new life!

Regards,
President Theo Evans

I have to catch my breath. I didn't know the president had anything to do with Comfort for Community. I thought he didn't like the program, and preferred deportation. At least, he's way more vocal about that option. Why does he pretend to oppose this one?

I look around the room. I don't feel alone, but that doesn't scare me. I'm pissed. I was dumb to think the government was done with me. Of course not. I'm Dinah, property of the government- just as I was property of my husband as Gertrude. I hate Gertrude. She was weak and trapped… and blonde. Am I really supposed to be blonde again? I love my dark hair. Why did I even do this?

I sneak in a quick shower. I'm bleeding pretty heavily. My head hurts. I'm exhausted, and my sides feel like someone is squeezing them. I've been feeling that way for a little bit. Part of me feels guilty, but I'm note sure why. I didn't want the baby. I never felt connected to it. I guess it's because I know how angry Richard and my parents would be, if they ever found out what I did to it. It's my last connection to them. Anyways, I know my new family will wonder about my new-to-them hair color. Thankfully, bleaching one's hair isn't seen as disobedience, and I'll only need to do this once.

Back in the bedroom, I drape a towel around my shoulders, then apply the dye to my hair to process. I hear a knock on the bedroom door.

"Dinah? You doing alright in there?" It's the woman.
"Yes, Ma'am. I'm fine."

There's no response, but I can feel a presence remain outside the door. I better open it. Indeed, the woman is still there. She's looking at me with a surprised, but pleasant look.

"What are you working on?"

"It was in my package, Ma'am." I think quickly on my feet. "My parents... they had a big storage garage. The agency put as much of my stuff in a box as they could. I know it sounds silly, Ma'am, but... looking in the mirror, I see my mom's brown hair. It hurts. Maybe this will help me move on better."

"Hmm. I wish you'd brought that up before ruining one of my favorite towels."

I look down at the floor. I'm trying to think of something to say, but nothing is registering.

She speaks up first. "Don't worry. The blonde hair will make you easier to marry off. Just don't make any more wild changes before discussing things with us first. Impulsive behavior hinders Simplicity. I understand that what you've been through has made you lose your way. There was no guidance. Women belong in the home, and you were without one for a short time. Your father and I will get you back on track for the Greater Good."

"Thank you, Ma'am."

"And you're going to have to make up for that towel."

"Yes, Ma'am."

"When you're done, clean everything up, and make yourself more presentable. I'm busy with some laundry. Dinner will be pot roast."

"Yes, Ma'am."

The woman pauses. She smiles all of a sudden, like a glitch- as if she forgot to do it earlier. She gives me another hug. I hug her back, waiting for the moment to be over. When she's done and walks out of the room, she leaves the door open. I know that's not an oversight. I pushed boundaries enough with my hair.

After my hair finishes processing, I take another quick shower. I comb my hair, then tidy up the bathroom. That takes care of that, but more boxes of hair dye are on the way. That, and I'm not sure what I'm going to do about those Enlightenment creams. I can't let anything pile up, and I can't just throw everything away.

3

"Wilful disobedience of our feminine roles is no different than trying to overthrow the country."

Last night was awful. They say rest makes everything better. I couldn't relax enough to do that. My stomach wouldn't stop fluttering, and my thoughts kept repeating. My chest was so tight, it was hard to breathe fully at times. I didn't want a single drop of blood on the sheets, so I went to the bathroom a few times to check my pad. I hope I didn't make too much noise.

I'm worried about those packages. My new parents are quiet about it now, but it's only a matter of time before they start asking questions. They'll want to open the packages with me... then for me... behind my back. Does the government have a plan for that? Will they have mercy on me if those people meddle? Most likely, no.

I think I miss my parents. I have no idea what happened to them, or to my husband. I doubt they're okay, and I'm sure I broke my mother's heart. One day, I hope she'll understand why I ran. It's strange. I'm so far away, but a big part of me still wants their approval, and craves affection from them. I don't feel the same way about Richard. Even without the abuse, I never really knew him, or wanted to be with him.

It kind of stings that his ultimate offense wasn't how he treated me. I could have told someone, but it wouldn't have worked out well. My own parents would have accused me of lying, because believing me would mean they'd have to admit their judgment was poor. I hate that I threw them under the bus, and had to compromise myself in this way. Now my husband is being made accountable for something he didn't even do. I'm the one who lied. I'm the criminal, and maybe this is my punishment. I'm always going to be looking over my shoulder. When my new parents find out about me, they're going to turn me in without question. The government, the media, and everyone else are going to make an example out of me. They'll all want me dead.

Knock, knock.

I sit up just in time to see the woman open my bedroom door.

"Sleeping in today?"

She's smiling- as always, but it's the kind of smile I'm most familiar with. She looks dead in the eyes and irritated.

"I'm sorry, Ma'am. I'll get up."

"Don't bother. I already made breakfast, and your father has already eaten. We understand you're dealing with some adjustments, but let's not stray too far. In order for us to find you a proper husband, we need to know what you're capable of, and what needs to be improved upon. Laying here tells us nothing."

"I understand, Ma'am. I'm sorry, Ma'am."

Her eyes stick to mine. "Did your previous household believe in self-care?"

"No, ma'am. Self-care neglects the Greater Good."

"Just checking."

She walks up to the foot of my bed and sits down, leaving my door wide open. I hold my breath as she begins to speak.

"Growing up, self-care was encouraged. The divorce rate was high, and the marriage rate was low. Women were especially lost. They opted for pills over children. They were aimless, promiscuous, and hoarding money while the homelessness and drug use rates increased. Turns out all that campaigning for self-care was a big scheme to encourage women to go against their natural roles, and destroy our country from the inside. Some people who are lucky enough to live here want to see everything burn. But our president listens, and so did I. I dropped out of college during his 1st term. A whole bunch of us did. He sees and respects us women as the backbone of society that we are. When we know our place, the community thrives."

"Yes, Ma'am."

"So the next time you decide to stay in bed a little bit longer, think about what history has taught us… What I saw with my own eyes. Wilful disobedience of our feminine roles is no different than trying to overthrow the country."

I can only stare at her. I knew it. I'm not safe here at all.

The woman leans in, still smiling. So… much… smiling. I know she wants me to believe she's being sweet and supportive, but I know it's a performance. I really want to let my guard down. I want to cry, and stop feeling scared. It's as if she can read my mind, because that smile she hung onto for so long finally left her face.

"Dinah, what needs to be done right now?"

"Um… I need to get up, make my bed, get dressed, then eat breakfast… Ma'am?"

"There's cleaning to be done downstairs. If you got up on time, your bed would already be made, and you'd already be dressed. We'd be eating breakfast right now."

"I'm sorry, Ma'am."

"Get dressed and make your bed. You may join me for breakfast after that, then I'll point you to the cleaning supplies.

You didn't help me prepare and serve the meal, so I won't help you clean up."

"Yes, Ma'am. Thank you, Ma'am."

***

Dining rooms make me anxious. Everyone I've ever found myself in has been surrounded by windows. They feel more like eyes. I peek out of one of them. Of course, these people have a pool. In a country full of drought, a pool… that no one swims in… is a status symbol. Women aren't even allowed to swim. It promotes too much leisure time, reducing the quality of our work towards the Greater Good. It's a distraction. Speaking of distraction, I still have food on my plate.

It's so colorful: purple grapes, over-easy eggs, crispy bacon, and a couple of fluffy pancakes. I've only taken a couple of bites. Nothing tastes bad, but my throat feels so tight, I have to force everything down.

"You're still working on that?" I somehow forgot the woman was sitting at the table with me. That smile found its way back.

I think of a quick lie. "Sorry, Ma'am. I'm careful not to eat too much. Big meals are best reserved for the husband."

"Good point. Go ahead and toss all that out. We're running a little behind, anyway. You need to clear and clean the table, then get started on the dishes."

"Yes, Ma'am."

She gets up and walks away. I immediately do as I was told. After throwing away all of the uneaten food, I clear the table. The empty sink is now overflowing. Wiping down the table and chairs is easy enough. Now, time to tackle the dishes. I grab a sponge and get started.

The woman enters the kitchen again. In the corner of my eye, I can see her heat up some olive oil in a red cast iron dutch oven on the gas stove. She gets a chuck roast, pats it dry, then sears it. The smell hits me instantly. I realize how hungry I am.

"Your father loves pot roast. He'll be pleased to eat it with you later."

"Sounds great, Ma'am." I kind of wish she'd stop talking. I want to be left alone, and I couldn't care less about that man. Actually, I have an idea.

"Ma'am, may I ask you a question?"

"Sure."

"That package, Ma'am... It had some instructions in it."

"Oh?"

"Yes, Ma'am, I... I have a responsibility that I need to fulfill."

"You have plenty of responsibilities here."

"Yes, Ma'am. It's just that... Before the fire, I... was already promised to someone."

The woman stops what she's doing. I can feel her eyes burning holes through my body.

I continue. "Everything happened so fast, Ma'am. The agency took over. I didn't want him to think I ran off, but I also didn't know where I'd end up. They contacted him for me. Told him I was being raised by another family, but he insists he still has rights to me."

"I don't understand. So, was that package from him?"

"Yes, Ma'am. He left it with the agency, then they delivered it here. They're not going to give him the address."

"Is something wrong with him? What did he send you?"

"Unfortunately, Ma'am, that would violate his privacy. I can't tell you, but I can tell you that he still sees me as his."

37

The woman shakes her head. "If you aren't married, then you aren't his. Your father has to agree to it as well. He'll move on. Is that what you meant to ask? If you still had to marry him?"

"Yes, Ma'am. I mean... It was my father's last wish for us to be married. Even though my father is no longer with us, his duty towards Simplicity lives on... through me. My path was already decided. Would my new father approve of me straying from the Simple path already paved for me? Wouldn't that make me disobedient? Denying my engagement and his letters is a form of free will. The decision can't be mine."

The woman nods. "You're right. We'll discuss it with your father tonight. He'll know what to do."

"Thank you, Ma'am."

What the hell am I doing? I already know what that man will say. He'll say that hanging onto the past doesn't serve the Greater Good. *He's* my father now. He'll tell me to ignore the suitor, then he'll want to dig into the package. I need to come up with something else. I take a deep breath, and let the words spill out.

"I'm pregnant."

The woman gasps. For the first time, she doesn't bother sounding pleasant. "The hell you are." She rushes over and leans into my face. "I have a couple of tests in our bathroom. Underneath the sink. Take one now."

I can't move.

"Right-flipping-now!"

I can't move fast enough. I run into their bedroom upstairs. It looks exactly like mine, but with a bigger bed. I don't know why I was expecting anything else. Running into their adjacent bathroom, I see the counter is full of hygiene products. Compared to the rest of the house, the products look like colorful jewels. The jewels expose individual preferences and necessities... personalities. No one ever told me outright, but it was well-understood that bathrooms were sacred spaces. As a kid, I got in trouble a couple of times trying to use my parents' bathroom. Guests aren't even allowed in another person's bathroom. For me, to be allowed in this space shows how serious the situation is.

I shuffle through the cupboard under the sink, and come across an unopened box of pregnancy tests. I grab one of the two tests inside the box, then urinate on it at the toilet. I wait. Suddenly, I hear loud footsteps. They stop just before the closed bathroom door.

"What does it say?"

I feel wounded and trapped. My mouth won't open. My only option is to open the door, and hand her the test. She has no reaction as she looks at it, and says nothing for what feels like forever.

Finally, she speaks. "It belongs to your boyfriend?"

"Yes, Ma'am."

"I see. Well, that's very disappointing. I had no idea you were so weak. That item in your womb is proof of your disrespect towards the Greater Good... and your father. He will not approve of a man who has touched you without his knowledge and permission. This proves a huge lack of discipline, Dinah, and a quickie marriage won't be a sufficient bandage for the complete disregard of your father's will."

"I know, Ma'am. I'm sorry, Ma'am."

"There is no way I can justify any of this. Your father can't know. You need to end things with that man. Is there a number you can call?"

"Yes, Ma'am. He left it in one of the letters, but... I don't have a phone. I'll need to use yours. You don't mind him having access to your number, Ma'am?"

The woman's face is full of panic. I'm trying my best not to crack a smile, as I can't believe I'm backing her into a corner.

"You're right. Nevermind. He might track us, or call when your father is present. He needs to be dealt with away from this house. Also, we need to take care of your... condition."

"Are you talking about adoption, Ma'am?"

She shook her head. "Adoptions are loud. A full-term pregnancy outside of wedlock is even louder. We need to be silent... for the sake of your father. He will want to marry you off as a virgin. If he knows he can't do that, then you're of no use to him. I always wanted a daughter. Finding you was the greatest thing to ever happen to me. I'll make the arrangements."

"Ma'am? Are you talking about- ?"

"A massage. As far as anyone will ever know, it's just a massage... to increase fertility. Your father will want you to bear many children, as I couldn't bring him any."

I'm so confused. The woman seemed so angry before. Now, she almost looks sad. In her moment of weakness, I feel confident enough to ask her something personal.

"Ma'am...Why me? Why didn't you adopt a boy? You could pass down the name with him. He could provide money, *and* you'd have grandchildren."

The woman's eyes are looking past me, into space.

"Then there would be *two* men in the home: one I couldn't provide a proper womb for, and another that would always be a stranger to me. When I heard your story, I saw myself. I was alone, too. You being here allows me to fulfill my purpose. I even told your father that. I begged him to take you in. Told him I'd be far more useful in the marriage with a daughter. I can pass down knowledge he doesn't have, and relying on a daughter-in-law as our eventual caretaker is a bigger gamble than hand picking our own daughter."

Disgusting. Again, she hugs me- gently, this time. I can hear her sniffling, feeling all kinds of sorry for herself.

"I can't lose you, Dinah. Your father can't ever know about any of this. Tomorrow… take the car for as long as you need to… as often as you need to. I assume you can drive?"

"Yes, Ma'am. Learned when I was 12. I used to help my mother with errands."

"Perfect. I'll take care of everything here, and that baby. You just get rid of that man. Your father will find you someone better. I will do everything in my power to protect you."

Her eyes begin to water. I feel nothing, but I have the car and I have her silence. Thinking about that releases all the tension in my shoulders.

4

"Past it is where *they* live."

    I can hear ocean waves. I look over at my alarm clock, and press the button. It's showtime. I get out of bed, and put on a long-sleeved, ankle-length floral dress with ballet flats. Flowers and bright colors are always a safe bet. I tie my hair back into a bun with a matching ribbon, then put on matching stud earrings.
    My mother used to tell me stories about how dependent women were on mirrors. She said they were accustomed to decorating themselves like tropical birds, and accentuating parts of their bodies with plastic parts. They focused so heavily on appearance, they put little focus on their duties. A social media influencer suggested that removing the mirrors from her home made it easier to focus on her behavior. Her video became so popular, Simples adapted the practice as part of their ideology. That didn't stop women from trying to dress nicely, though.
    I don't think there is an actual rule book for Simples. Our ways of life are passed down orally within families, and we just happen to run into the same types of people. I always thought of

that as weird, because if our way of life is ideal, then why can't everyone know about it?

There's my mind trailing off again. After making my bed, I head downstairs to help with breakfast. I roll my eyes at how little Simple women are supposed to care about our appearance, but we have to go out of our way to make meals look spectacular. Silverware and dishes can't just be clean. They need to match, be expensive, and be placed in a specific manner. Food can't just be cooked and seasoned well. It needs to be plated as if it was a work of art. I've never known a man to inspect the placement of a fork, the price of a plate, or whether or not a bowl of soup was picturesque. I'm not sure why we do this, but I do not intend to be the one who doesn't.

The woman's voice is soft. "I hear your father coming downstairs. Get in position."

We both move to the kitchen entrance, ready to greet with warm expressions. We look so excited to see him. This is so stupid. After all that, the man breezes right past us to his seat at the head of the table. As soon as he sits down, he stuffs his face. We just stand there. No 'thank you', 'how are you?', 'good morning', 'this tastes great'... We're no different than the windows. We're either open or shut, letting in light to shine on someone else. Enough of this. This wasn't the outcome I wanted. There has to be something else out there... something I'm not allowed to see. I want to see it, and I want all of this to burn.

A snap of the fingers. "Dinah."

I come to. The woman is looking right at me.

"He's gone. I'll clean up. Here are the car keys. Do whatever needs to get done, but be back by 2pm. You'll need to help me with dinner."

"I have to grab some things first, Ma'am."

"That's fine. The less I know, the better. Same on my end. The less *you* know, the better. Just be quick about it."

"Okay, Ma'am." I almost forgot to ask. "By the way, Ma'am, are there areas I should avoid?"

"The Lowlands at the bottom of the hill. You'll see a nature preserve that surrounds the whole base. Past it is where *they* live. If you must go downtown, keep your face forward, and get through all of that without stopping. You'll soon hit a whites-only freeway entrance."

"Okay, Ma'am. Thank you, Ma'am."

She then gives me a cold glare. "If you are not back by 2, I will not defend you."

"Yes, Ma'am."

5

"You're either brave or stupid."

    I run upstairs to fill a large purse with as much as I can: some tubs of Enlightenment cream, leftover dark foundation, a washcloth and a water bottle. I can't help but chuckle as I leave the house and lock the door.
    I put the key in the ignition. I think about driving away as far as I can. Only, the tank is half empty, and I have no money. If I decide to take a chance anyway, I will anger my current family, as well as the government. I will have no one and no place to turn to, and be more useful dead. I need to be patient. My game plan will take some time, but it will pay off.
    I pull out of the driveway, and get a good look at the neighborhood as I pass through. I was so in my head coming from the airport, I didn't bother before. I guess that's because I knew- deep down- I'd see nothing new.
    Just like my old neighborhood, there are Simple flags everywhere, and every home is huge. The land each home sits on is even larger- covered in fruit trees and gardens. I guess I'm supposed to be impressed, but I think only men could ever be.

They're signs of a man's wealth, power, and ridiculous need to take up space. I see nothing but prisons for women to fill and keep clean. I'd rather see them burn.

Just then, it hits me: my hair. I don't know how I managed to completely forget that I dyed it back to blonde. I park on the side of the road, and open up the glove compartment. I see a colorful head scarf, and a few hair ties. My mom kept a head scarf in her glove compartment, too. In case her hair misbehaved while on errands, she had a way to look more presentable. I tie my hair back, and secure as much of it under the head scarf as I can. That settles that, but it's not a permanent fix. I start the car back up, and get going.

Driving down the hill, I approach the nature preserve. I only saw it through the corners of my eyes before. The woman was right. The trees seem to wrap all around the bottom of the hill. The dense greenery brings back good memories of being in my outdoor learning pod.

I remember tuning out sometimes to watch insects crawl or fly, or hear the birds nearby. I could see a world beyond my own, and I wasn't lonely. All of the other girls were also promised to suitors at a young age. While we were prepped to become wives and mothers at home, the pod was our space to think about anything else. We could speak freely and informally with each other. We could build friendships on our own- based on our own interests. It was the closest to independent any of us were.

I pull into the entrance of the nature preserve, then park in the lot. I'm the only one here, but it doesn't feel that way. I take a thorough look around before I begin applying foundation and bronzer to my visible skin. I'm trying my best not to lean on anything, or smear on my clothes.

I love what I'm seeing in the rearview mirror. It feels like another person smiling back at me. She's not stuck in the house- cooking and cleaning thanklessly. The expectations put on her are different. She can make her own decisions, and speak freely. She can get dirty, and use her hands to make whatever she wants. She's invincible; she's free.

 I start up the car again, then drive towards the Lowlands. I feel as if I'm leaving Earth, and venturing onto a whole new planet. There are no more mansions, or huge yards with gardens and trees. Instead, I see clumps of buildings, and many more people on the street. I've never seen so many black, yellow, brown, and red people before in my life. Well, outside of movies and news stories. This doesn't feel like real life, though- more like an exhibit.

 Mom told me they prefer living separately from us. That's why Evans supports segregation. It's for their benefit... their own form of Simplicity. However, misinformation spread. Many accused the government of forcibly segregating them. As a form of retaliation, they're known to violently protect the spaces they inhabit. Simples became the bad guys, instead of the people who supported their way of life in the first place. It's logic only they understand. Mom said that's why I never met any of them before. It was safer to keep our distance.

 Just then, the most amazing thing catches my eye. I slip into the parking lot, because I need to take a closer look. It's unlike anything I've ever seen. It's a giant pool, and it's not at someone's home. It's out in the open, and full of people. There are even waterslides and a diving board.

 The women have me staring. They're hardly wearing anything at all. I can see whole legs, stomachs, backs, arms, and even cleavage. Some are wearing their hair down, but talking to men who don't look like husbands. Other women are gathered in small groups- not being accompanied by men at all. What could a group of women have to talk about amongst themselves and outside the home? Why are none of them being shamed? Why aren't they at home cleaning, or prepping for dinner? Some of them are wet. Did they swim? *Can* they swim? Leisure time takes away from the Greater Good. Do they not care… or not know? What do they know that I don't? What goals are they meeting right now? Who benefits?

There are children present. What skills could they possibly be obtaining? All I see is talk and play. There's so much laughter. Those are things I could get away with when my parents weren't around, but their parents are present. That has me feeling a little angry, but I'm not sure why. *They* are the aggressive ones, and they live by a whole set of rules I do not understand. This is going to be a hell of a lot harder than I thought.

My heart is beating so fast right now. I can hear Mom's voice. She'd be so mad at me for not focusing on household duties.

I remember her basically telling me, "Being a wife and mother is natural, safe, and beneficial to the country. Our purpose is in the home. Women who work outside the home are intentionally neglecting their purpose. They only have themselves to blame when things don't work out."

I don't think I can do this, but it's too late to give up and drive back. I almost jump out of my seat when I see myself in the rearview mirror. I forgot about the damn makeup and scarf. I also forgot how covered up I am. My skin tone won't stick out, but my clothes will. Oh, well. I'm in it now.

"They can't see you, Gertrude. They don't know you and can't see you. Get out of the car, and make something happen."

I slowly open the door handle, then take even more time getting out of the car. I'm screaming inside of my mind, but keeping my face still. I see a restroom up ahead. It doesn't even say *Black, Brown, Yellow, Red* or even *Non-White Restroom*. Just *Female Restroom*. I move carefully, peeking at everyone around me. There's still so much laughter, and they're loud when they speak. Here, instead of men taking up the land, everyone takes up space with their voices. I've never witnessed women and children having any sort of equal footing with men. I've never seen women show so much skin without being whipped and ostracized. This world carries no tension. None of these people could care less about me, or anyone else around them. I'm the one obsessing.

I walk into the restroom, and go into a stall to sit down on a toilet. I need some time to think and breathe. How am I going to do this? I can't just walk up to people. They'll ask questions. They'll sniff me out right away, then that will be the end of it. After a while of gathering my thoughts, I finally come up with something.

I flush the toilet that I didn't use, then walk up to a sink I don't intend to use. I take a deep breath, then pull out a tub of Enlightenment from my purse. I place it on the counter in front of me. I'm not trying to make a bunch of noise, and bring too much attention to myself. No matter. Everyone is looking at me right now.

A black woman comes up to the sink next to me. Her eyes are stuck on the label. I'm trying my best to pretend like I don't notice, but I'm also having a tough time pretending to be occupied. I can't wash my hands, and I can't look up. All I can do is fiddle with the sink knobs like an idiot. I anxiously want some kind of response from the woman, but I get none. She says something like, "Two" under her breath, then hurries away.

Well, that worked out great.

Just then, a brown girl walks up to me. She looks about 14. I'm distracted by her bathing suit. So much of her skin is exposed by the cropped halter top and shorts, but she isn't ashamed. She's completely unbothered, and giving me the most intense eye contact I've ever received from a near child.

"Is that real?" pointing to the bleach cream. "You're either brave or stupid."

I think my heart stops for a moment. "What?"

"Ever since that law passed months ago, no one touches the stuff."

"Law?"

She gives me a confused look, then steps back. "You don't know what I'm talking about?"

I shrug. What else can I do?

She sighs. "You used your I.D., right? No one can buy bleach cream without one anymore. They say it 'prevents minors from buying', but I know two full grown women in jail right now. That info led cops straight to them. They were arrested for *intent to defraud*. Can you believe that shit? You don't even need Twos with a law like that."

That's the second time someone brought up Twos. I have no idea what that's about. I try to think on my feet. "They think we're stupid."

"Yes, you are. I wouldn't go back home, if I were you. How'd you even get that brand? That's prescription-only."

I don't know what to say.

She leans in. "Why are you so covered up?"

I shrug. "Just how I was raised."

"Hmm. You here by yourself?"

"Just some friends."

"Where are they?"

"Waiting for me."

"You plan to swim in that?"

"I don't swim."

Silence. I look up to see all of the other women in the bathroom looking at me with the same intense expression. I knew it. They can smell me.

All I can hear is my heartbeat. "Look, I... I guess I blocked that law out of my mind. It's so messed up. Before it passed, I hoarded a whole bunch of this. All under the radar."

The girl pauses. "What's your name?"

"My name?"

"You walk in with your body all covered up, and some bleach cream no one else can get- even *with* I.D. I know people in jail over that stuff, but you're out here with a tub all out in the open. What are we supposed to think?"

I have no idea how to answer. Is she upset that I don't have a bathing suit on? Is she jealous of me having the Enlightenment cream? Am I about to be robbed? Made fun of? It definitely doesn't look as if anyone wants to buy anything from me.

The girl repeats herself. "Your name? What is it?"

"Dinah." The name is meaningless to me anyway. They can have it.

The girl nods, then addresses everyone else in the restroom. "We all heard that, right? Anything goes down, we know Dinah was behind it, and we can put a name to a face."

As everyone nods in agreement and carries on with their day, I put the cream back into my purse.

The girl looks back at me and whispers, "How much of that do you have?"

"Excuse me?"

"How many do you have?"

"A lot."

"That law passed 3 months ago. Some of that stuff is gonna go bad."

I wish she'd just rob me already, because I'm ready to go back home.

She asks, "How much do you want?"

I'm so relieved to be wrong. "How much do you have? In cash?"

The girl looks into her purse. She has an unsure look on her face, but I can clearly see the multiple $20 bills in her wallet. I'm amazed to see someone her age with that much money on hand.

"$80," I say. "For one."

"For one?"

I grin in response.

"Okay. How long will you be here?"

"Can't say." Truthfully, I want to leave as soon as possible.

"Will you be here tomorrow?"

"No."

"If I can get others to buy from you, will you be here tomorrow?"

"Not likely."

"Okay. I'll take one."

I lead the girl towards a stall. Loud enough for others to hear, I say, "I only have one extra tampon on me. Sorry I can't get you more."

She understands. "That's okay. Thanks for looking out."

After we delicately make the exchange, she closes herself inside the stall, and I walk on. I feel pretty good about myself, but that was a lot. I decide to head back to the car.

Nearly back to the vehicle, I feel someone close behind me.

"Miss."

I turn around. It's a brown woman holding hands with a small boy. At least, she has a sarong on. Not every woman here is trying to be as naked as possible. The whole place makes me feel unclean. Maybe that's where my anxiety is coming from.

"Was that really your last tampon?" she asks.

"Um, yeah. Sorry."

"Could you… look again? I have cash."

Whoa. Is this really happening? Is my plan working? Around here, it seems as if I'm needed, and I can offer so much more than my womb and obedience.

"How much cash?"

The brown woman looks nervous. I can't believe it. *I'm* making her nervous.

She says, "$20."

I shake my head, because I can. "I can't help you."

52

"That's all I have on me, but I can get some more."
"I'll give you half an hour. Price is $100. Look for Dinah."
"Okay."

No argument. She didn't sneer or yell. She just walked away with her little one. She took me at my word, because I'm the one with authority. Here, with this product, and in my new skin, I'm not just a woman. I can be out in the sunshine, and talk to whoever I want. I can have my own money. I can call the shots, and be intimidating. Maybe this is why these people fight so hard to live separately from Simples. They're onto something, and want to keep us in the dark. Whatever it is, I'm going to take a big piece of it for myself.

6

"I have cash on me."

I check my phone. It's 12:45 pm. I need to hurry up, because I'm starving. I sold all but one tub, but that's okay. I did a whole lot better out here than I thought I would. Heading back to the car, I feel a tap on the shoulder. It startles me. I turn around and immediately gasp.

He looks about my age- my actual age. His skin tone is very similar to my makeup, and I love his short, brown curls. I want to run my fingers through them. He can hardly look me in the eyes, but I soak up the tall, lean image of him. His dark green swim trunks go down to his knees. There are black flip-flops on his rough-skinned feet, and a light blue bath towel over his broad, naked shoulder. All of that cloth is so lucky to touch his skin. I wish I could. The sweet, earthy scent coming from him is intoxicating.

The last time I felt this way, I had the biggest crush on a friend's brother. I was 9, and he was 12. There was no use in exploring or expressing my feelings. In fact, that would have complicated our paths. Love is reckless. People make it sound so wonderful, but a lot of mistakes were made over the years because of it. Simple families help their children find the right match, so such mistakes can be avoided. Abiding by that match is a sign of respect. A lack of respect is grounds for ostracization.

Physical attraction is deceptive and selfish anyway. I never felt any sort of attraction towards my husband. I was just performing a duty, fulfilling a role. When I was married off, I finally understood the lack of affection from my parents. I didn't reach out to Richard. I didn't need hugs, kisses or attention. I didn't mind when he was away. I was able to see sex as mechanical. Even now, I don't miss him. I'm not worried about him, because Simplicity always protected him. I couldn't fight back. I couldn't tell my parents that they were wrong.

Are my feelings toward this guy in front of me right now wrong? He wasn't chosen for me, but I feel the strong attraction I've been warned against. Am I experiencing something natural, because I'm brown right now? *Am* I brown right now? Color codes are based on looks- not genetics, so the government would see me as brown. Everyone around me sees me as one of them. As a Simple, I can't choose who I want to be with. I have to consider the Greater Good. I don't have to consider it now. Maybe that means I am allowed to think for myself.

He looks up at me. I can feel my eyes widen, so I can process more of the beauty of his dark, brown eyes.

"You're Dinah, right?"

"Yes." My voice breaks. I clear my throat, and try my best to look as if I couldn't care less about him. Truth is I've never been so drawn to another human being before. I've never been approached by a man in such a way, either. I'm used to overbearing, yet dismissive men. This guy feels warm and vulnerable, and he has features I've never seen up close.

"I have cash on me."

For a second there, I had no idea what he was talking about. I forgot about the pool, the restroom, and the fact that I was headed to the car. I forgot the car isn't mine, and home is up the hill. I also forgot why this guy already knows my name. I'd like to know his name, but I can't be too forward. I better stick to business.

I have him follow me to a nearby oak tree. There's no fruit growing off it. That's another thing that strikes me about this place. There are just… trees… for everyone… without food on them. It's weird. I like that he's following me from behind, too. Normally, I'm the one who follows. I wonder if he's sneaking a look at my body. I wonder if he has the same urge to touch me. Maybe he needs a signal. I turn around and look deep into his eyes. I smile, pushing myself to breathe normally. He looks around us plenty, but hardly at me.

"How much?" he asks.

I don't want things between us to start off on the wrong foot. If he buys from me today, maybe I'll be able to see him another day. I need to keep the cost low, but if it's too low, he might think there's something wrong with the cream. I'm also curious to know what he can afford.

I keep a straight face. "$100."

He nods and pulls a wallet out of his pocket. I can't keep my eyes off his hands. He takes the bills out of his wallet. As I exchange the tub of Enlightenment, I pretend to overreach accidentally, and caress my fingers over his hand before taking the money. His skin is so rough and warm. I look at him and smile, but he's still so much more invested in our surroundings. After a moment, and without a word, he just walks away. I can only let him, but I can't keep my eyes off his curls.

I get back in the car, and drive around the neighborhood. Thankfully, I don't have to go far before I find a generic hair care store. I park in the lot. Walking towards the store, I see mannequin heads with wigs at the display window. The one that catches my eye right away is a curly, brown updo. I step inside. The brown woman at the counter addresses me with a warm expression, but is busy with another customer. Perfect.

    I make my way towards the wig. I reach out my hands, and close my eyes as I gently feel the curls. It's almost as if I'm touching *his* hair. I have to have it. With a smooth and quick motion, I snatch it off the mannequin head, then shove it into my purse. I look back and around. No one is looking back at me. No one is pointing me out. How did I just get away with that?

    My heart is beating faster as I head back to the entrance. Just as I'm about to leave the store, the counter lady says something.

    "Thank you for stopping by."

    A big, toothy grin spills onto my face. "Thank you."

7

"I'll make sure you're thoroughly clean before any man ever sees you."

    The idea of driving back to the house is depressing. I'm going from laughter to silence, people all over the streets to empty yards, and *him* to the Clarks. Like before, I stop at the nature preserve. Thankfully, the parking lot is as empty as it was in the morning. I put the head scarf back into the glove compartment, and carefully wash off my makeup. Before leaving, I decide to bury the washcloth.

    I pull into my new parents' driveway, and walk up to the door. Before I have a chance to unlock it, the woman opens it.

"You must have gone far."

"It's about 1:30, Ma'am. Still half an hour left. Is there a problem, Ma'am?"

"I guess I wasn't expecting you to be gone that long. Come inside."

    She moves over, so I can enter the house. Then, she closes and locks the door.

"Everything good now?"

"Yes, Ma'am. He got the message. He wasn't too happy about it, though."

"But it's all handled?"

"Yes, Ma'am."

"Good. Now help me make dinner. Your father is getting pot roast tonight."

This will be my third dinner with the couple. It will be the second time we've had pot roast, but she announces it as if it's a unique treat. I'm guessing she married a picky eater, and needs to excite herself about eating the same meals all the time.

She carries on. "You might want to change your clothes, too. You're a little sweaty. Maybe put on some perfume to cover that up?"

"Yes, Ma'am."

The woman pauses, but her eyes are still on me. I feel like I have to say something.

"And you're right to be concerned, Ma'am. I'm sorry for being gone so long, and the day has been quite warm. I shouldn't be so unkempt. I'll clean myself up. Thank you for allowing me to use your car, Ma'am."

"You're welcome, Dinah. Now you're home where you belong, and I made an appointment for that massage. I'll tell your father it's to prepare you for marriage. We should marry you off as soon as possible, so that makes sense. Your father will be pleased with that plan."

I can feel my shoulders tense up. "Yes, Ma'am. How soon is the appointment, Ma'am?"

"Next week, and don't worry. I'll make sure you're thoroughly clean before any man ever sees you."

"Ok, Ma'am. Thank you, Ma'am."

I walk back to my bedroom. I try my luck by partially closing the door, then stow away the cash I made in my undergarment drawer. Almost $500. That's something, but not enough. I have way less time to work with, too. I thought I'd get to finish the summer, and maybe spend a couple of months in the learning pod before talking about suitors. Next week is around the corner. Since the woman plans to spin the massage to her husband as marriage preparation, I bet she already has a suitor in mind. Correction: her husband does.

It's a good thing I can hardly remember the couple's names. It won't be long until I'm sent to live with my new husband. The thought of that terrifies me. I owed my parents, but I owe these parents even more. They're not motivated by obligation. They *wanted* to save me, and are using their resources to keep me on my path. Plus, the government is keeping tabs on me now. What am I going to do?

8

"He must have followed me home."

I wake up and have to go to the bathroom right away. I'm still spotting a little, but not enough to fake a miscarriage. That would avoid needing a *massage*, but it won't stop me from getting married.

I want to go back to the Lowlands. The woman was willing to lend me her car when she thought I was tied to another man. Maybe... I'm still tied to him. Maybe my attempt to get rid of him didn't work. She wants to get rid of the imaginary baby quietly, but she can't do the same with the imaginary husband. A man fights for his property. That's it! Now, what in the world am I going to do with that information?

I get myself dressed, and do the whole song and dance for breakfast time. At this point, I think the man sees me as more of a servant than a member of his family. I don't know why I expected anything else. I don't know why I keep doing that to myself. I'm sure the woman doesn't see me as a daughter, either. She has her moments of sweetness, but then she snaps out of it. She's more like two separate people, and I can't trust either one of them. Whatever. I'm leaving anyway.

***

"Kitchen is clean. I need you to work on the laundry while I fill up the tank and get some groceries. Wash, dry, fold, and put away. Every last bit."

"Yes, Ma'am."

The woman gathers her keys, then heads out the door. I wait until she pulls completely out of the driveway. Then, I run up the stairs, and go straight to the man's office. The door is always closed, so I'm excited to see what's in it.

The result is underwhelming. There is a desk, a chair, the same bland wall color, and some typical office supplies. Why does he always have the door closed then, and why is no one else allowed inside? What are we not allowed to see? Whatever. I grab a sheet of paper and a pen, then get to work.

I write the following in the sloppiest way possible:

I know you live here. I know you have my baby. I'm coming for it, and killing anyone who gets in the way.

I smile at my work. I close the office door behind me, then shove the pen I used down to the bottom of the kitchen trash bin. I crumple the letter in a ball, uncrumple it, then put it in the mailbox outside. No sign of her car. Perfect. Plus, our neighbors' homes are so spaced out, I doubt anyone sees what I'm up to.

I immediately make my way to the laundry room. The washing machine is already done, so I start transferring the clothes to the dryer. Then, I put some linens in the washer. I can hear the front door open.

"Come help with the groceries!" The woman sounds exhausted already.

I rush to the front door, but she calls me over to the kitchen.

"I'll grab the stuff from the car. You put everything away."

"Yes, Ma'am."

I do as I'm told. Turns out there were a lot of groceries. After the woman brings everything in, she helps me put the rest away.

"What are we making for dinner today, Ma'am?"

"Beef stroganoff," she replies, grinning from ear to ear.

I'm relieved that we're not having pot roast again, but I'm at the point where I'm really put off by the woman's pleasant expressions. I'm convinced she only smiles at me to put my guard down. I choose not to smile back anymore.

"Sounds good, Ma'am." I proceed with my plan. "I was wondering, Ma'am... "

"Yes?"

"Well, since you'll be so busy in the kitchen, and I'll have breaks between loads... Would you like me to get the mail later for you, Ma'am?"

"Thank you for reminding me. I forgot to get yesterday's mail. Normally, I'm on the ball, but I was preoccupied with yesterday's events. I'll go get it. You can return to your duties in the laundry room after putting everything away."

"Yes, Ma'am."

I can't tell if I'm scared or really happy. I don't remember there already being stuff in the mailbox, but I wasn't paying that much attention. Should I have been? Is the woman going to recognize her husband's paper? Is the letter going to look like a child wrote it? Is she going to laugh the whole thing off?

I hear the front door open and close. No words. No foot stomps. Maybe the letter blew away somehow. Maybe the woman already threw it away.

"Dinah." The woman's voice breaks my concentration. I turn around. She's standing at the laundry room doorway. "We have a problem."

She hands me the letter. I pretend to be mortified, trying hard not to curl the ends of my lips.

"I don't understand, Ma'am. He must have followed me home."

"You told him about the baby?"

"No, Ma'am! The agency must have. They poked and prodded me when I was there. Maybe he asked questions, and they didn't hold back."

The woman raises an eyebrow. "They never said anything to *us* about you being pregnant."

"I told him to let me go, Ma'am. I belong to another family now. I thought he understood that."

"Well, he didn't. We can't let your father see this letter, and we can't have the noise of a police investigation. We also can't have him showing up at the house. I thought you said everything was handled."

"I'm sorry, Ma'am. What are we going to do?"

Okay, so maybe this isn't going to work. I expected her to be *worried* about me- not mad at me. The last thing on her mind right now is to give me the keys, and have me on my way to wherever I want. I messed that possibility up. What was I thinking?

After a long pause, the woman finally speaks. "Let's sit down." She takes my hand, and guides me over to the living room couch. We sit, and she gives me that same damn smile.

"I know you tried, Dinah. Words are all we have, and men don't take them very seriously. I know it's frustrating. I can't fault you for his reaction, but I can't help you, either. I can't be associated with this, and neither can our home. He needs to be lured away from here and quietly handled. Tomorrow morning, as soon as your father leaves for work, take my car and go to him. Will you know where to find him?"

"Yes, Ma'am."

"Good. I'll have something for you when you leave. Keep it to yourself. You'll know what to do with it, and you'll need to discard it after."

"Ma'am?"

"He won't listen to you, Dinah. You need to make him listen, and- believe me- it is possible to be loud without making a sound."

She stares off into the distance. I don't know what to make of any of this. I'm not even sure if she's still mad at me. She looks back at me, and holds me close. Even though I'm not sure what I think of her, I kind of like the affection. I can't let that distract me, though. I still plan on running away. Her hugs won't protect me from the man her husband is going to force me to marry. Now, the woman is crying.

I sigh. "Are you okay, Ma'am?"

The woman tries to talk through her tears. "You're the best thing to happen to me. I'm so sorry this is happening to you. I'm sorry about your family, and I'm sorry that man is treating you this way. I wish I could do more. I really do, but your father would be furious. We'd both be out on the street, and the entire community will shun us. I can't let that happen. I once had a suitor like that man. I told my mother how he was, but she sided with him. I found a way, though. After him, my parents met your father. I won't let you struggle, Dinah. I am here for you... as best as I can be. With him gone... and that baby... you will have a good life- like me. You will always be well provided for. I promise."

I'm numb. I still feel no connection to her, her husband, or this home. All I can think about is running away, and that boy in the Lowlands. I want to be able to choose who I want to be with. I want to be outside, but not just to run errands. I want to swim and let my hair down. I want to be taken seriously. I don't want to be in danger of losing my house for speaking up. I want a life entirely different from this woman. She thinks she's helping me by keeping me in line. I want to be out of line. I want to make noise. I can't have any of these things as a Simple, but I can have it all with brown skin.

9

"Are you spying on me?"

As soon as the man leaves for work, I get in the car with my wig, foundation, water bottle, and a new washcloth. I bring the last few tubs of Enlightenment cream I have on me. A new supply won't be shipped until next month. That gives me enough time to think of another excuse to head back to the Lowlands.

As directed, I look inside the glove compartment. I see a dark pink pistol, and I assume it's loaded. I guess I should be grateful, but I'm kind of annoyed. What kind of sense does this make? That woman was in tears about not being able to call the police, but she's okay with sending me out to kill someone? Sure, the guy is totally made up, and I'm in no danger. She doesn't know that, though. She's more concerned about losing the house and her standing in the community. I have a crisis, but she's thinking about herself!

I drive to the nature preserve. This would be an ideal place to lure someone and stash a body, but I won't have anything to bury. Should I bury something else to save face? Maybe I can say he was scared enough by the sight of the gun, so there was no need to kill him. Should I bury the gun, in order to hide any connection to the totally made up crime? Probably not. Something tells me the gun will come in handy someday. I decide to keep it in my purse, then put on my makeup and wig.

    I then take a good, long look at myself in the rearview mirror. The brown features make my blue eyes pop. I love the texture of my hair, and even my clothes suit me better. I look healthier somehow, and far more interesting.

    I drive straight to the pool. I missed the oak trees and the noise. Women in the Lowlands get to wear all kinds of colors on their bodies, hair, ears and feet. I'm so jealous. I want to be colorful, too. Growing up, wearing bright colors, or too many accessories was considered noisy. Women are to dress nicely and match, but they can't draw too much attention to themselves. Otherwise, Simples will look down on you. No one is looking down on these women. I'm certainly not.

    I step outside of the car. As soon as I do, a few women look over at me. I wasn't noticed like that yesterday. Seems I've made a name for myself. The colorful, beautiful women see something in me worth paying attention to. I'm flattered; I belong.

    I make my way towards the restroom, when I see someone familiar approach me from the side. He taps me on the shoulder. That sends electrical impulses throughout my body. Not only is he here, but he sought me out, and he needed to touch me. The force of his finger lingers on my skin. I wonder how the rest of his body would feel against mine.

    I smile at him, but I want to do so much more. He's wearing the exact same trunks, flip-flops and towel he did yesterday. It's like we're reliving the moment we first met. Also like the first time, his eyes are everywhere but on me. I know he's only around for the Enlightenment. I'm still thrilled to see him, and flattered that he remembers me.

I walk him back to our oak tree. This time, I walk beside him. I think about holding his hand. Instead, I just glance at it from time to time. Maybe he'll take a hint, and grab mine. He doesn't. I ask for the same hundred dollars I did yesterday. Again, he is able to pay. No flinching, no complaints. After the exchange and another accidental hand caress, he's ready to dart off again.

My new, golden skin gives me confidence. Here, black, brown, yellow and red people can speak freely. I am one of them, so I can do the same. A Simple man would disapprove of me speaking out of turn, but maybe this guy will respect me for it.

"Wait."

He looks back at me, confused. "You can check. I didn't short you."

I'm so thrown off by his eyes and the deep sound of his voice, I can hardly recall what he said. I'm also smiling like an idiot.

"No, I mean…What is your name? You already know mine."

He looks around. "I'm… from around here."

With that, he runs off to meet up with another young female. She's beautiful, too. Her maple syrup skin, those moisturized coils, and a colorful one-piece. I love her clear-framed prescription glasses, and large woven bag. Everything about her looks so well put together, yet effortless. Meanwhile, I'm out here practically in a potato sack down to my calf. The young man shoves the tub of Enlightenment in the young woman's bag, then kisses her on the lips. They look so happy together, walking into the pool area.

I feel betrayed. For the brief time I've known him, it felt as if we had something. He remembered me, and needed me. He took me to the oak tree, because he wanted to be near me. There was never any mention of anyone else.

I can still feel his fingertip on my shoulder. I've imagined my whole body up against his so many times, I swear it feels as if it happened. That other girl is a distraction. I understand more and more why marriages are arranged. Left to his own devices, he thinks he's with the right person. That girl isn't marriage material. I'm not showing off my body. I'm not wearing bright colors like a bird. Yeah, I was jealous of that before, but maybe my bland look is my strength. In my world, I'm average. In this world, I stand out. People who stand out are important.

I gasp. I totally forgot that I have two more tubs on me. I can sell them, or use them to lure the boy out of the pool area. That's going to be really hard to do, since there are so many people. There's no way to get his attention without getting everyone else's, and I don't want to be on that girl's radar. I know I'm already on *his* radar.

Maybe he's performing for me right now. He wants me to chase him. That would make sense. He approached me twice. It's my turn to put in some effort. I keep my eyes on him. I imagine my gaze pulling him towards me. He's going to turn around and come back to me.

Just then, he and that that girl turn around. That's exactly the sign I need. There really is a deep connection between us. The girl appears to be looking around. Maybe she forgot something, but I don't really care. He's holding her hand. I imagine my hand in his instead. While the girl lets go, and runs towards the parking lot, he stays put at the gate. I focus on his eyes, hoping he'll look back.

He does! He sees me still standing at our oak tree, and he actually holds me with his eyes. I knew it. I start walking towards him. He actually begins walking towards me. As soon as we catch up to each other, he moves in even more. This is the closest our bodies have been. I wonder if he's trying to hold himself back from fully embracing me. I bat my eyes, giving reassurance that I want him near.

He points towards the oak tree… *our* oak tree. My mind is swirling with possibilities as he guides me there. Now that the girl is out of the way, he can't hold back his feelings for me any longer. He needs me. Any moment now, he's going to tell me that he loves me.

Finally, he says something. "What's up?"

Well, that wasn't quite what I expected. "What do you mean?"

"Are you spying on me?"

I'm so confused. Spying? He can't feel any warmth in the way I look at him? He thinks I'm up to no good? That girl of his must be all kinds of toxic. He's all guarded. Maybe that's why he can't pick up my energy. He just needs a little patience.

"I forgot to tell you about a special sale this week."

"*After* I already paid you? I got as much as I wanted anyway."

"I could give you a little money back, or I can give you an extra tub."

He's looking around. I know he's looking for that girl. Was he always looking around for that girl? Did he ever see me at all?

I roll my eyes. "Nevermind. Go on."

"Hold up. I'll take the extra tub."

"Wait. Really?"

"Yeah." He holds out his hand.

I chuckle. "Okay. I just need you to answer one question first."

He groans, and brings his hand back. "What?"

"What's your name?"

"Why do you want to know my name?"

"It's important for me to know the names of all my clients. I would have asked you sooner, but you keep running off."

He looks at me for a long minute- staring at my face, then he scans my body. I'm not sure what he's looking for, or what he really wants to say, but I keep smiling. He doesn't smile back. He's so lost in his head.

"Abraham!" The girl calls out, walking back from the parking lot. The young man perks up.

"Fuck," he says under his breath.

Abraham. It's repeating in my head, and I cling onto every syllable. The name is so unique and strong. It fits him perfectly. I think about him pinning me up against the tree with his strong arms. I want to be engulfed in his scent, and feel his soft lips against mine. I want his lips and hands to travel all over my body, as he whispers about wanting me for so long. Except, his eyes are already pretty occupied. He looks ready to run off again.

I sigh. "Is that your...?" I have no idea what to call her.

"Yeah."

"She's pretty."

"Yeah. She is."

His eyes aren't meeting mine. He's so preoccupied. Maybe he's eager to meet up with that girl, but he's not going anywhere fast. I think he prefers to be here with me. He's drawn to me, and willing to be so vulnerable. I bet he's not vulnerable with her. He puts on a show of affection with her, but has a deeper connection with me. I can tell he wants to tell me something. Maybe he needs me to open up that door.

"What's wrong?"

He shrugs. "Don't worry about it. I'm good. Anyways, I gotta go."

I watch him run off to his beautiful, bifocaled girlfriend. They kiss and head back to the pool, hand-in-hand. I'm not even worried. Moments ago, he was alone with me. He wanted to be at our special spot, and he scanned my body. Men don't bother to associate with women they're not interested in. That girlfriend of his is a temporary setback. He's unhappy with her, but he probably

72

has trouble leaving her. It's not like they're married, but I do understand. He just needs a little push.

10

"I don't know what happened to that man, but after he was dealt with, the whole thing was swept under the rug."

    I manage to sell the rest of my Enlightenment in the restroom, then head back to the always-empty nature preserve. It's been a long day, and I'm exhausted. I'm already daydreaming about returning to the Lowlands as I take off my wig, and clean off all the makeup. What kind of excuse can I make to go back? The crazy ex thing is tired. Oh, no! I completely forgot my new mom was pretty much telling me to kill him, and bury the gun.
    Obviously, I'm not killing anyone. Maybe I can get away with telling her that I was able to scare him away. No more letters, and no more need to worry about him. He got the message. I'll tell her I buried the gun too, but I really intend to keep it handy in my purse.
    Now… What am I going to do about that massage? I have no idea what to expect, so I don't know how to give a convincing performance. The masseuse will know I'm lying about being pregnant, then blow my whole plan. I can't go through with it. I

can't decide against it, either. The woman thinks she's helping me. She thinks I'm soiled, so she wants to clean me up. She's being kind.

Kindness is so strange to me. It's talked about as if it's such a wonderful thing. It has nothing to do with what I want. It's about what others want for me. Kindness and expectation are interchangeable. Maybe that's why I'm so weary of it.

***

I pull up to the driveway. Like before, as soon as I get to the door, the woman is waiting for me.

"Are you okay?"

She looks really flushed in the face, as if she had been crying. I don't have the energy to explore why, but I'll use her energy to my advantage. I keep my voice calm, while adding stress to my face.

"I'm fine, Ma'am. May I come in?"

"Of course." She steps out of the way.

Walking inside, I tell her, "Scared him off, Ma'am. Doesn't want too much trouble. Your item is well hidden, too. He's not a factor anymore."

"Good. Are you sure you're okay?"

"Yes, Ma'am."

I need her to press me more. I bet the whole situation has her on edge. She can't vent to anyone else. Her pressing me also makes it so I don't seem too forward with what I want to talk about. The benefit of dealing with Simples is that when you've dealt with one of them, you've dealt with them all. They only know one way to be, so I'm confident I'll be able to mold her just fine. I have so far.

The woman shakes her head. "You don't look fine. Please... sit on the couch."

"Don't we have dinner to tend to, Ma'am?"

"Yes, and the bathrooms, but all that can wait a few minutes. I need you to sit down."

We walk over to the living room couch. I can feel her anxiety. I'm sure she can feel mine, but she probably thinks we're on the same plane. I'm only anxious to get this over with.

She says, "I know how you feel. I've been there, only my action was more than just a scare. I know that was a lot to ask of you, and to have you go through that alone. I'm sorry for putting you in that situation."

"That's okay, Ma'am."

Is she really apologizing? My mom never apologized to me. No one ever has. Now, this woman is? I still plan to leave. She's not going to guilt me into changing my mind. She wants to kill my imaginary baby, and force me into marriage. She's not a good person. If she was so sorry about what she put me through, why did she put me through that in the first place? I'm so irritated right now, but I need to hold that in.

"Does he know about what you did, Ma'am?"

"Your father? Of course not. When the body was found, the community blamed it on another Simple. I don't know what happened to that man, but after he was dealt with, the whole thing was swept under the rug. I got to start a new life. I was lucky."

"That is lucky, Ma'am."

"Perhaps."

I catch this woman very often looking off into the distance or on the floor. That's a good thing. She can't tell how hard I'm trying to hide my disgust right now. I can't talk about my struggles with her, because that would make me a selfish burden. I'm supposed to sit and listen to hers though, because it's a sign of respect.

The woman wipes tears from her eyes. "I want to show you something."

She gets up, and leaves me on the couch. I watch her walk upstairs, and hear each footstep. She's going to her room. I can't make out much beyond that. A few minutes pass before I can hear her walking back to the staircase, and back to me. She has something in her hand.

"Is that a Bible, Ma'am?"

"It is." She sits down next to me, looking fondly at her book. "It's my mother's. She held onto her faith until the very end. Asked me to hold onto it."

***

My parents told me we used to go to church. We stopped going shortly after Evans became president- back when I was 2. Most Simples turned their backs on organized religion around that time. My dad told me that no one could agree if God was vengeful or loving, if salvation was earned through belief or work, how one should dress to church, what is metaphorical and what is literal, or what should be avoided. He told me that he knew what he saw and heard from Evans. Evans was real.

He said, "I've had a more tangible relationship with him than God. I've seen him grow alongside me. His words are clear... unmistakable and loud. I was one of the people to lift him up, and we're being rewarded for it. I *know* this. I am certain of my role, and how to serve the community. I know we will thrive for as long as we praise him, because we will see and feel what will happen the very moment we don't."

I was told to avoid anything and anyone having to do with organized religion. My parents were convinced that those who looked up to anyone besides Evans were unpatriotic. In fact, they were a threat. Turns out a lot of Simples feel that exact same way. I don't remember the president ever telling people to stop practicing their religion. I guess he didn't have to.

***

"Does father know, Ma'am?"

"He doesn't. The words are meaningless to me, but the book itself is very comforting. It's like she's still with me."

For such a devout Simple, the woman is very confused.

"Why are you showing this to me, Ma'am?"

"I… I don't know, actually. I guess… It's what bonds all of us. Isn't it? We women are nothing without our secrets."

I nod, because I can't think of anything to say. My mother never shared any secrets with me- much less, knew any of mine. She was just a mouthpiece for my dad. She knew her role, and she fit it completely.

"You inspire me, Ma'am."

The woman's face lights up. "I do?"

"Yes, Ma'am. I assume there's a Simple Watch around here, Ma'am?"

"Of course."

"I'd love to participate, Ma'am."

"Really? I've inspired you to do that?" She looks so flattered.

"Yes, Ma'am. Out of appreciation for how you care for me… I want to put effort into caring for the community. Helping you with the housework is very valuable, Ma'am. Both your knowledge and my involvement in the neighborhood will attract the right suitor."

"We'll see what your father thinks. The Simple Watch will take away from your household duties."

I have her right where I want her. "I understand, Ma'am. It's just that… I've been out of the house, driving around twice now, Ma'am… in *your* car. I'm sure the neighbors recognize your car, and are curious about me. You know as well as I do that they will approach Father with questions- not you, so we'll never know what they're saying. We'll never know what kind of questions Father will spring on us, and how to keep our stories straight. We could tell him I've been driving to the store, but what if people say they never saw me there?"

The woman doesn't have an answer.

I carry on. "This is becoming greater than us, Ma'am. We're straying away from the Simple path. I mean, you were lucky to avoid suspicion once. Seeing me at the meetings, and investing in the safety and welfare of the neighborhood will keep their eyes off of you. We'll both be redeemed."

The woman's eyes get bigger, but she still doesn't have an answer.

I make something up, confident that she won't know any better to call me out. "I stopped by the grocery store today, Ma'am... just to walk around and calm my nerves a bit. I saw a flier on the community board. Meetups are every Friday- women only, of course. Men meetup on entirely different days."

"Very good."

"I'd love to go, Ma'am. Have you been?"

I already know the answer. Simple wives can't speak freely to people outside the household. I bet she hardly looks up while checking the mail. I imagine her keeping conversation short and formal with grocery store clerks. She has no idea who lives around her. When she murdered her ex, she probably fell deeper into the Simple hole out of guilt. She needs to work twice as hard to appear loyal. So, of course, any sort of social activity outside the home- even if it does serve the Greater Good- is out of the question.

Other than older Simple women with adult children, many single women join the Simple Watch program. In fact, a majority of female participants are single Simple women looking to gain favor by the right suitor. It gives the illusion of choice, because ultimately fathers are the ones who orchestrate unions. Once married off, women abandon the program for their fruit tree-covered prisons adorned with Simple flags.

"I... I haven't. I never had any interest in participating. My role is in the home."

"My role will be in the home too, Ma'am. In the meantime, I need to find a husband. If I grew up around here, and other families were comfortable enough with me, it would be a different story. I'm running out of time."

"You're right, Dinah. So... the next meeting is in a few days?"

"Yes, Ma'am. Thankfully, meetings are done by 2pm."

I made up a random time. Thankfully, the woman is nodding along with everything that I'm saying.

"Fine. Take my car then. We'll talk to your father during dinner today, just in case he doesn't approve."

"I know you'll make it right, Ma'am. Should I get started on the upstairs bathrooms or the downstairs ones?"

"Um..."

Minutes ago, the woman looked ready to cry. Now, her eyes are all over the place, and she's tightly wound up. I don't think she wants me out of the house. She needs a doll to take care of, and make her feel good about herself. Me being exposed to other women, and speaking on issues within the community will lessen her influence over me. Women have so little influence to begin with. Plus, she knows she will lose me to a man. Until then, she has control. At least, that's what I need her to think.

11

> "Since I'm keeping a little secret of yours, can you keep one of mine?"

Friday can't get here fast enough. For the past couple of days, I've been writing Abraham's name on hidden areas of my body. Since know one else knows, it feels exciting. With each stroke of the pen, it's as if he's touching me. I can hear his baritone voice, and smell his body when I close my eyes. It feels as if I'm washing off his stench when I shower at night, just to cover myself in him again in the morning. I want to always belong to him. I need him. We have something, and I'm sure he misses me. A kiss would be the natural next step. He just needs to know I'm ready.

I gather my essentials: my wig, makeup, washcloth, and water bottle. The gun is still in the glove compartment. Arriving back at the pool area, I have trouble holding in my excitement. I can't wait to see Abraham again.

When I step out of the car, a red girl walks up to me.
"Excuse me… Do you have an extra tampon I can use?"
"No. Sorry."
"Still headed to the bathroom?"

I shake my head. "Don't need to go."

"Later today, maybe?"

"Maybe."

The girl smiles big and walks away. I'm not getting any more supplies for another few weeks. I figured Enlightenment would be popular, but I had no idea how popular. Next time I sell, I'm increasing the price.

I walk to the sacred oak tree and wait. I can't see Abraham anywhere. It hits me that he might not come to the pool every single day. I certainly don't. I might stand here for hours, and never see him. After all, he has enough Enlightenment to last him the rest of the month. Maybe I won't even see him in a month's time. Maybe he gave up on me. Maybe he married that girl, because he thought I abandoned him.

I am relieved to suddenly see him within the crowd. I'm not sure if I'm hallucinating, though. He's walking towards me, and looking right at me. His girlfriend is nowhere in sight. He's not dressed for swimming. His cologne arrives before he does. As I inhale him deeply, he speaks.

"You're hard to find."

I could feel my face flush. He's here for me? Just me? He's been looking for me long enough to think of it as hard? I knew it. He loves me, and he's ready to tell me.

"Heads up…"

I bat my eyes. My heart is racing. "Yes, Abraham?"

"I'm moving next week."

My whole body deflates. I want to fall to the floor, but I'm trying with all my might not to. "What? Why?"

"Last time I saw you… you had free Enlightenment for me? I forgot to take it. Do you still have it?"

"I… sold it. I.…"

This isn't at all how I pictured this scenario. Is he still being guarded? After he took all that time to find me, he still can't

82

admit his feelings for me? Why is he acting like the only reason we talk is because of that damn skin bleach!?

He sighs. "Oh."

I see I need to steer the conversation to something more productive. "That girlfriend of yours... I bet she's really going to miss you."

"Yeah, um... I'm moving pretty far. Long distance never works, so..."

"You broke up?"

"Yeah." He's finally free. Now I get it. He sought me out, because he needed me to know that.

"I'm so sorry, Abraham."

I want to move in closer and hug him. Before I get a chance to, he says, "Since I'm keeping a little secret of yours, can you keep one of mine?"

"Anything, Abraham."

He takes a deep breath. His eyes are on the floor. "I'm... I'm Blended."

My words come out like vomit. "So am I."

Abraham gasps then grins. "I wasn't sure. Really?"

"Yeah."

"Funny thing is I thought you were a Two at first..."

I'm hearing that number again. I still have no idea what it means. "What made you think that?"

"The way you dress. No one knows you, and you just showed up with a bunch of expensive, highly regulated skin bleaching cream to sell. No one has disappeared, so you're definitely not a Two."

"So... you trust me?" I can't help but smile. "I trust you, too."

I finally hug him, pressing my body up against his as much as I can. I nestle his neck, and deeply inhale his scent. His grip on me isn't limp or defensive. It's tight. I bet he is loving the sensation of my skin. I think I can hear him softly crying, too. This moment means as much to him as it does to me. This is the most realistic love I've ever felt.

I sneak a little kiss on the cheek. He lets go of me, perhaps not to seem so overeager in public. I can respect that. He's a little sniffly, and his eyes are moist. It's so endearing. I'm just as overwhelmingly happy.

"What was that for?" he asks.

"I'm just so happy to know another person like me. It feels good to be honest."

He sighs. "It's just that... My parents are breaking up. I look more like my dad. He's staying, but I'd rather be with my mom. She keeps a low profile out here... obviously... but now she doesn't have a reason to. That's why I've been buying the creams. I want to resemble her more, so I can live with her in the Highlands."

"Is she a Simple?"

Abraham shrugs his shoulders. "What choice does she have?"

"And you? All that trouble to be with your mom when you're going to be married off soon?"

Abraham gives me a puzzled look. "Married off? Only Simples do that shit, because they're obsessed with purity. Are your parents arranging your marriage or something?"

Purity? Purity of what? Merit? *Obedience* is what I always thought Simples were obsessed with. Fathers want their children to marry those who positively impact the Greater Good. When I think of purity, I think of how women's bodies are supposed to be before marriage. It's only part of the equation. After marriage, she doesn't need to be pure anymore. She must be fruitful. Meanwhile, obedience is expected by all of us at all times. How does Abraham know about any of that, anyway? I never knew anything about him or his people.

I try to shake off my irritation. "Um… Of course not. I mean, since your mother will be a Simple, and you plan to live with her, you'll have to do what they do."

"Maybe."

"There's no 'maybe' when it comes to Simples. You're in or you're out."

"Then I guess I'm getting married up there."

My mind scrambles to think of a way to convince my new dad to marry me off to Abraham after he moves to the Highlands. Only, that would require me to reveal the truth about my color code. I can't do that. Besides, Abraham fell in love with a Blended girl- not a Simple girl. I still want to leave the Highlands, too. I don't belong there, and neither does Abraham.

"Well," I take his hand, because I need to touch him. "Your secret is safe with me, Abe. I'm sorry for what you're going through. I do wish you well."

"Thank you." He half smiles.

"I mean that. You deserve a lot."

"Thanks."

I can feel him want to turn and walk away, but I can't let him. I give him another hug. He feels a little limp this time. I know his mind is wandering. I can't lose him so quickly. I decide to go for it, pressing my lips against his. Instantly, my whole body tingles. Nothing and no one else exists. He leans into my kiss, pressing my body against our sacred oak tree. His hands move about my body. I'm ready to completely give myself to him, and honor him for the rest of my life.

"Let's go to my car," I whisper in his ear.

For some reason, that is when Abe chooses to collect himself. I could feel him want to pull away, but I hold on and press my lips harder. What we have is special. I understand he's going through a lot, but that's no reason to turn me away. Our bond can overcome anything. He resorts to pushing me off him. He's so stubborn. I'd be more upset, if I wasn't already so stimulated.

Before darting off again, he says, "We can't. I'm sorry. I shouldn't have done that."

Now I'm the one who has to collect myself, but it's hard. My eyes travel around him as he leaves. I relive the pressure of his long, defined arms around my body, and his lips on mine. I love his broad shoulders and wide palms. I can still smell his hair and skin. I'm compelled to follow him, but my body isn't moving.

Maybe this is a test. Maybe he needs to know how dedicated I am to him. By staying still, I'm giving him control… expressing faith in his word and leadership. I was wrong to want to control over him. He reminded me of my place. I understand. Romantic love does make one selfish. True love is through duty… my duty to him. I know he's going to return to me. He's not really leaving. After all, he went through so much trouble to find me in the first place. He loves me, and we both want a different life. This is our chance to live it together. All I need to do is prove how patient and faithful I am. Then, he's finally going to love me back. The thought of that makes me smile.

12

"Wanted?"

The massage is scheduled for today.

All weekend, I thought about what I could do to prevent it. I assume that if I don't look really uncomfortable and bleed a lot, they're going to think something is up. My period hasn't come yet, and the heavy bleeding from my abortion is long since gone. The dryness is going to raise eyebrows. It's been over a week since I had an abortion, so I doubt my hormone levels are already back to normal. I can't count on a negative pregnancy test after everything is said and done. So what do I do?

The man has already left for work. The woman has her car keys ready in hand. She insists on driving me to and from, because she says I'll be in no condition to do so myself. How *kind* of her.

She stepped back when it came to murdering my imaginary ex, because she didn't want any of that to trace back to her. Never mind what could have happened to me. My super-secret imaginary abortion is fine, though. She can be all over that, because she has a level of authority. When it came to the ex, as crazy as I made him out to be, *he* was the one in control. He was the one whose comfort she considered. The only way she could factor out his feelings was to remove him entirely. What if I wanted to keep the baby? What if I actually loved my ex, and wanted to stay with him to honor my imaginary father's approval?

I follow the woman to the car. As we buckle up, she gets all sentimental again.

"How are you feeling, Dinah? I'm sorry for not asking earlier. Between the household and your father, I get so distracted. Sometimes I think I'm in survival mode. My mind zeroes in on things. I don't want you to think I'm not considering your feelings. If you need to pull me aside to talk, I can listen. I want to listen. It's only your second week here, and so many heavy things have happened."

"I'm fine, Ma'am."

I want to roll my eyes. She waited until now to say something? To ask me how I feel? She wants me to open up to her? Give me a break. She's feeling guilty, and wants me to stroke her ego with applause. That's all this is.

"One more thing, Dinah... When your father isn't present, you can drop the 'Ma'am'. I'm your mother, yes, but... When I was little, that title was reserved for employers or strangers. Somehow... parents became both to their children. Yes, having children is a duty. Passing them along is a duty. I don't see you as a duty, Dinah. I see you as someone I love very much. Please call me 'Mom'."

I'm mostly tuning her out. "Okay."

The woman looks at me, as if she wants to say more. We're obviously in no hurry to get to the appointment. Maybe I can use this to my advantage. I think I finally have a plan, and I wonder why it took me so long to come up with it.

"So... Mom... Can I tell you something then?"

"Sure." She starts the ignition, and begins pulling out of the driveway.

88

"I think I'm being punished."

"Punished for what?"

"I'm not sure, but I don't think my body wanted me to have this baby."

"*Wanted?*"

"I mean… I think my body bled it out last night."

The woman quietly pulls back into the driveway. She turns off the ignition. I try my best to keep a straight face, because I really want to smirk.

***

I know that my mom- my actual mom- bled out a few babies. She said she wasn't being a good Simple wife, so her body didn't allow her to become a mother. As soon as the babies began to form, her body flushed them out. Her body ached, too. She was tired. It was as if her body scolded her for even trying. She told me that my birth was proof she fulfilled her wifely duties, and duties as a citizen. After I was born, however, her body was quick to humble her. She wasn't allowed any more children.

I can easily apply that to me. As far as my new mom knows… I lived, despite my whole family. I started off being careless with my chores in her home, and I gave my body away before marriage. I threatened my arranged husband with a gun. Now, I plan to abort his baby. I have influenced the woman to opt against honorifics, and lie to her husband. I'm a bad Simple. It should make perfect sense to the woman why my body won't allow me to carry a baby.

I bet that's why she doesn't have a child of her own. Her body punished her for what she did. She has her husband and her house, but she needed a child. I'm the best thing to happen to her. She tells me all the time. She needs me as proof of her goodness and usefulness. Then, she turns around and jinxes my life. Now, I can't have children. What a great storyline.

Of course, I don't believe any of those reasons why women bleed out. It seems like another way to keep us in line. I mean, how do we know it's not the man's fault?

***

I can sense the woman's panic.

"Last night?"

I slap on a pitiful expression. "Yeah. I've been reckless and selfish. I know you say you love me, and want to protect me. I need to be a good Simple, but I've been bad. I've been sneaking around, and spending too much time on personal business- instead of what needs to be done in the home. I want to redeem myself with the Simple Watch, but it's too late and not enough. I think this massage was the last straw. Yes, I had premarital sex, but I was with the man I was going to marry. I was being obedient. Turning my back on him doomed me. I'm not going to be worth carrying anyone's child."

I turn my head away, holding back fake tears. I know the woman is feeling so racked with guilt, she's not going to ask me for proof of bleeding out, or for another pregnancy test. I'm not even worried. I just hope she doesn't take too long to say something, because my acting already has me feeling ridiculous.

The woman holds me to cry in her arms. I can only muster enough energy to sniffle, because I'm more annoyed than anything. I'm surprised to hear her crying. She's so weak. Why is she always crying and spacing out? Isn't she happy... *lucky*, as she put it? I shouldn't be getting to her this easily.

"Let's go inside," she says finally. "There's a lot to be done inside the home. Keep going to those Simple Watch meetings. I'll use grocery money to get you a burner phone, so we can keep in touch privately… in case things change, and we need to keep your father out of the loop. You're going to be fine, Dinah. I will personally see to it that you are, because the Greater Good needs you."

"Do *you* need me… Mom?"

"I do."

She hugs me again. I have her wrapped around my whole finger.

13

"They reassigned her color code to red, and renamed her."

    Another package has arrived. It includes the same cold letter, and the same amount of supplies. Although, I hope to make twice as much money this time.
    Since I've had nothing to sell, there's been no point in going to the pool. I only drove to the neighborhood once to get more foundation. I thought about stopping by the oak tree, so I could run into Abraham. I do miss him. Maybe he's still hanging around. I didn't hear about any new people moving here in the Highlands. Then again, I know nothing about my neighbors.
    I like to think Abraham is still in the Lowlands, and me not being there is driving him crazy. My husband used to stay out late after work sometimes. He never told me where he was, or what he was doing. He was allowed to come and go like that. Being a good wife, I never made him feel guilty. I never asked questions, and I was always patient. Now, the tables are turned. Abraham has no idea where I'm at, what I'm doing, or when we'll see each other

again. I'm the one allowed to come and go, and he has no choice but to wait. Deep down, I know he is.

During so-called Simple Watch meetings, I hang out in the nature preserve parking lot. I have no idea why it's always empty, but I'm not complaining. The solitude is nice. While there, I like to put on my wig, and paint my face. I've been experimenting with colors on my eyelids, lips and cheeks. I can't recognize myself; I find that exhilarating. I like to have the windows down, so the breeze and sunlight can touch my brown skin.

Caressing it, I like to imagine not being able to wash it off. I can stay in the Lowlands, and be a part of a community that sees a lot in me. I'll be loved and accepted for who I am, and valued for my potential as a person- not just a wife and mother. Women in the Lowlands have options, and they're not shamed for the choices they make. Their lives are perfect. I want what they have.

***

It's Friday. Time to head out to the Simple Watch again. I grab my makeup, wig, washcloth, water bottle, and supply of Enlightenment. I check to see if the still-loaded pistol is in the glove compartment, then drive to the nature preserve to get dolled up. Abraham isn't going to be able to hold himself back. That's fine with me, because I'd rather have his touch than his money.

I pull up to the pool area. When I step out, I expect the crowd to stop in their tracks. It's been so long since I've been present. I provide a popular service. Plus, I look especially pretty. Only, no one cares. There's less laughter than before, and less people. What happened?

I walk to the women's restroom. No one is making a big deal about my return. I wasn't missed? Was I wrong to think I was respected? I'm so disappointed. A couple of women ask for Enlightenment, but they're skittish. Everyone's energy is way off. I have a few hundred dollars in cash in my purse right now, but I don't feel much satisfaction. This place isn't how I remembered it. Maybe I'm wasting my time here.

I step out of the restroom. Walking back to the car, I instinctively look at the old oak tree. Good thing, because standing right next to it is my Abraham. I've been away for 3 weeks. He indeed thought about me, and he waited for me. He really is mine.

I run to him. "Abe!"

As soon as I'm within reach, Abraham gently covers my mouth with his hand. The sudden feeling of his fingers spread over my lips catches me off guard, but I'm not afraid. My dream is coming to fruition. He is so overcome with his affection for me, he can't contain himself. I look deeply into his eyes, reassuring him that I feel the same way. He removes his hand from me, then presses his index finger vertically over his parted lips. A sweet confession is about to escape.

"I'm not buying anything today."

I giggle. "I know."

"We need to talk." His voice is stern. I move in a little closer, giving him greater access to my body.

"Something has happened," he says.

"I know. Oh, Abe. Are you sure you want to talk here like this... all out in the open?"

He sighs. "You're right."

He moves to the other side of our oak tree, entrusting me to follow behind him. I'm so giddy, and eager to hear what he has to say.

"The news isn't talking about it, but everyone else is."

My smile drops. "Wait. What?"

I don't get it. He waited for me to come back. I have. We are together at our oak tree. Why bring anything or anyone else up at this moment? Why can't Abraham express his feelings with words as well as he does his lips and hands? Does he want me to become ravenous?

Simples want submissive, quiet women. Parents do all of the dealings, but suitors are pretty forthcoming with their expectations. Here in the Lowlands, no one is pulling the strings, and men are like puzzle boxes. That must be why women out here wear less clothing. They speak assertively with their bodies. Maybe that's what I need to do.

Abraham, again, sighs. "And they're not going to, because she's supposed to be invisible anyway."

"Wait a minute… *She*? Did you get back together with that girl?"

"What are you talking about?"

"Who are *you* talking about?"

He pauses and studies me. I'm scrambling to figure out what just happened.

"Let's try this again," he says. "I'm talking about Abril. You heard what happened, right?"

I glare at him, trying not to flip out. Why is he concerned about some other girl? Is he dating her? Is he trying to make me jealous right now? It's kinda messed up that he sought me out, and lured me to our sacred oak tree just to antagonize me.

Abraham nods at my lack of response. "Abril is just 5 years-old, and she's Blended like us."

In an instant, I can feel the heat leave my face. I take everything back. I never should have doubted him, but it's his fault for not being straightforward. His mind games are exhausting.

"She lives on my block. She was kidnapped a couple of days ago. I'm pretty sure a Two is behind it."

Maybe I can make him tell me what a Two is, because I'm still in the dark. "Really? Why do you think that? I'm sorry, I… The girl's name sounds familiar, but I haven't heard much about what happened."

"Really? Wow. Well, we know the guy who kidnapped her is part of the Simple Watch up in the Highlands."

My heart stops. It takes me a moment to remember that I have nothing to do with the all-male chapter. I wouldn't know the guy, and I'm pretty sure he doesn't know me. I'm safe. Oh, that's right. I'm not really a member of the all-female chapter, either.

"Hey. You okay, Dinah?"

"What?" I have no idea how my face looks, but I'm sure it looks pretty flushed about now. I'm flattered he can see the changes in my mannerisms, and thinks to check up on me. That's something only a deep connection can do. "I'm fine. Keep going."

"Okay. Well... He knew about her parents, and bragged to everyone about what he did. Somehow all that information made it down here. There has to be a spy."

Hmm. So a Two is a spy? The name makes no sense, but whatever. I guess that explains everyone's weird attitude. What happened to the little girl sounds awful, but she might have left willingly. Maybe the family doesn't want to admit she preferred elsewhere. I can understand that. I bet I'm a missing person case in my hometown. It could have been made to look like a kidnapping, too. Maybe she's hiding in plain sight like me. I'm sure she's fine, and- more than likely- better off.

"Social media?" I shrug.

He shrugs back. "Sure, but how did he learn about Abril? That she's Blended? How was he able to kidnap her from her home? Something's not right. Someone from the inside helped."

"Oh, goodness."

"And you know that Comfort for Community Law? It really is a relocation program, and it involves a lot of fucked up shit."

Fucked up shit? How would he know? My past life was fucked up. My whole life was decided for me when I was a child. I was never seen as a person, or allowed to think of myself as one.

Everything revolved around other Simples- including my worth. I needed to fall in line just to be invisible. The most attention I ever got was from my husband. That man used to beat me for no reason, and I was forced to procreate with him. I was hurting, but couldn't turn to anyone. Comfort for Community saved me, and those packages are helping me make money. I'm becoming financially independent. I'm being exposed to different people, and seeing a whole new way of being. I never would have experienced this as just a Simple. Abraham has no idea what he's talking about.

He leans in, and keeps his voice down. "The guy who kidnapped her said they did a bunch of tests. They reassigned her color code to red, and renamed her. Said she goes by Nicole now. She was adopted by a whole new family, but he didn't say where. The nurse even asked if Abril's parents were expecting another kid. They're missing now, too"

That's because they were arrested. They were harboring an illegal person. I'm sure that another Blended baby would have extended their jail time. My husband and parents were also arrested. Was it all framed to look as if they're missing, too? Part of me wonders why it's better to have the public think people are missing instead of in jail, but whatever. It's done.

Abraham is still on it, though. "Thankfully they weren't, because that nurse was going to order an abortion. Evans made a big deal about how evil abortion is, but he's using government funds to kill Blended babies. On the same day Abril was kidnapped, a cop was at her house. That part I saw. I was driving by when it happened. The parents weren't arrested... no cuffs or anything. They were laughing about something in the front yard. It was like they knew each other. No one has seen the parents since. Nothing in the news, no social media posts...nothing."

"Does anyone know about *your* parents?"

Abraham appears a little annoyed by the question. "I don't think so. They've been lucky this long. They're still separating, though, and it doesn't look like I'm going anywhere. I don't think I'll ever be light enough to pass off living with my mother. The whole thing worries me."

"Why?"

"Let me worry about that. Anyway, there's safety in numbers. I don't know about you, but I know a few other Blended people. We all want to do something. The authorities around here act like they never heard of Abril. It's why I've been looking for you. I wanted to make sure you were okay."

This is my chance. I smile at him with my eyes, then give him a big hug. He holds me back, but very softly and briefly. He's not fully present, but he didn't force me off of him either.

"You should join us, Dinah. We need all the help we could get."

I can hardly process what he's saying. All I sense is the roughness of his defined chest, and the musk of his sweat. I think I can feel his heartbeat. I wonder if he can feel mine, too.

"What do you say?" he asks.

My mind is still cloudy. "What are you talking about?"

"A fucking revolt."

A *what*!? I'm trying to make a new life for myself. I don't need anything holding me back. Besides, I don't even live here, and I never even knew Abril. His reality is not my reality, and the Comfort for Community program isn't what he thinks it is.

"I... I don't know, Abe."

He backs away from me. "Why not?"

"You want to call a lot of attention to this, then fine. The only change you'll see is being labeled a public nuisance. Even worse... you'll be outed as one of the Blended, then they'll get your parents."

Abraham shakes his head. "One of my friends has an apartment. I've been thinking about moving in with him, so things can be a little more discreet. I have a better chance of being able to move in with him in this neighborhood, than with my mom up the hill anyway. Yeah… I think that's what I'll do. I love my dad, but he's kind of a stranger to me. You know what I mean?"

"I'm sure your girlfriend will be happy to know you're still in town."

"She's not my girlfriend anymore. She's with someone else."

"Oh. That's too bad. I'm sorry."

"What's with you, Dinah? Are you in or out?"

I'm really taken aback by how stressed Abraham is. He's so personally invested in a stranger, despite having so much of his own stuff to sort out. I can relate to putting my emotions and needs on the backburner, so others can be tended to. Such a thing was never required of any man. Yet, Abraham puts himself in that position. I can't wrap my head around that part.

Thankfully, I don't foresee me needing to do much, or a huge time commitment. Abraham and his friends can have their little protest, then we can focus on our time as a couple.

I nod. "I'm in."

"Good. We're meeting tonight". He hands me a handwritten note. "That's the address, and my cell phone number. Get rid of that paper as soon as possible. If you know any other Blended people, bring them too."

"I know of one, but she might be too scared to come."

I hate lying, but I feel backed into a corner. I have nothing valuable to add to the conversation, and I want to appear as interested. I need to be valued in his eyes. I thought I already was, but our foundation feels shaky. If I don't strengthen it, I'll lose him. Now, how am I going to be available for this meeting?

"Do what you can. See you tonight."

As he gets ready to dart off, I lunge at his cheek with my lips. I glow at the sight of him, but he's blank-faced.

"Look, Dinah... That one day... It was a mistake. I'd say I was weak, but that's a messed up thing to say. I see you as... a friend, and want to respect you as one."

I smile. "But friends don't kiss."

"Did you hear what I said?"

"I heard you."

Abraham turns away from me, but I keep my eyes on him. I can tell I'm making him nervous. He could run, but he isn't. He's just standing there, allowing me to be in complete control. It feels good. Maybe this is what Simple men fear. They told us such behavior was unnatural and chaotic, but I've never felt more whole. We have to be beaten, and separated from everything. We're led to believe our power comes from our ability to fulfill the roles they made up. They don't want us to know how complex and capable we are. We're human beings- not appliances.

I give Abraham the space to run off again. He does. That's fine, because I know I'm on his mind right now- not Abril.

14

"Come straight home when it's all over, then let your father know everything."

Ring... ring... ring.
The woman picks up. "Hello?"
"Mom, it's me."
I'm in my car, still at the pool. It feels surreal to speak to her with my makeup and wig on. It's as if I'm not really talking to her at all. Someone else is taking over, and I bear no responsibility for the outcome.
"Are you on your way?"
"Not yet. I'm going to be late."
"That's a problem, Dinah. You need to be home soon."
"But Simple Watch is running late. I wasn't able to get a hold of you until now. It's an emergency."
"What's going on?"
"Something is brewing. Did you hear about that Blended girl?"
"Your father did hint at one being caught. I'll admit I wasn't paying too much attention. Her parents broke the law, and

she was made accountable for their carelessness. That's why committing such a crime is so horrendous. Innocent children suffer."

"Well, the people down the hill are mad. They're blaming the Simple Watch, and they want to retaliate."

"Oh, my. Thank the Greater Good for Twos."

"Yes." I pause, unsure how I want to proceed with the conversation.

"They are proof that our methods work. Simplicity works. Some people love to complain, though. They say color codes are problematic, and living separate lives denies basic human rights. The truth is that organization leads to Simple, harmonious living. Being in Simple Watch, you get to see the inner workings of how society remains so peaceful."

"How did you learn about Twos, Mom?"

"I was there when the movement emerged. Twos empowered red, black, brown and yellow people, while the media obsessively labeled them as oppressed. The people in the Lowlands are actually quite happy, and free to live how they want to. Only a select few create chaos. Twos weed them out, so the community can thrive."

From what I've seen, I do agree with her. There's a calm out here I never experienced around Simples, and women have a lot more freedom. I need to focus on the task at hand, though.

"Who is the Two that outed the girl's parents?"

"I've never known a Two personally, and I've never learned of any names. I know they exist, though. The right people know about them. Thanks to them, you have a heads up on a possible rebellion. Come straight home when it's all over, then let your father know everything."

"I will."

"Great. You're doing incredible work, Dinah. You will certainly attract the right husband."

"Thank you, Mom."

"And I'm very proud of you. I'm hanging up now."

"Okay. Bye."

"Bye, honey."

Click.

I take in a deep breath. I'm so torn, because I do love Abraham, but I have to tread carefully. I'm still working on saving money, so I can run off. I want him to come with me, but if he causes a big scene, I'll have to leave him behind. No matter what, he will always be the love of my life. I'll always want what's best for him. I want what's best for me, too.

In fact, I think I figured out a way to postpone any possible marriage arrangements. After word of the revolt drama spreads, Simples will want more soldiers on the ground. If I'm stuck at home, serving a husband, I'll be unable to serve the Greater Good during a crucial time. I know the Clarks will approve. The people will put me on a pedestal up on that hill, while I continue to earn a living down here. Before I know it, I'll have enough money to leave, and find someplace better.

I start up the engine, and make my way over to the meeting. I look forward to seeing Abraham again.

15

"Abraham, where did you find her?"

    I pull up to a light coral-painted restaurant with lots of windows called Soul Code Kitchen. I don't understand the meaning behind the weird, unappetizing name. The parking lot is tiny, but there's plenty of street parking available. I decide to try my luck with the small lot. Walking towards the restaurant, I see Abraham at the swinging entrance door. He glows at the sight of me.
    Opening the door wide, he says, "You came."
    "Of course, Abe."
    I look around. The restaurant appears so much bigger from the inside. The walls are decorated with old photos of what appears to be the neighborhood. I can recognize some of the businesses, and one photo- in particular- sparks my interest. Behind some homes is a big hill with the same trees as the nature preserve. Although, it's not just a ring of trees. The whole enormous hill is covered with them.
    A few people are seated at a table: a guy and girl sitting next to each other, and another girl sitting opposite from them. I

have no idea who any of them are. We all look about the same age, though- late teens to early 20s. From the outside, we'd easily pass as a group of friends. Are they friends? Am I already sticking out to them? At least, I have Abraham. I hope to be able to sit next to him.

When Abraham does sit, he does so next to one of the girls at the table. She's coded black, and wearing a yellow tank top. Her coarse curls are pulled back with a colorful bandana- making a voluminous, short ponytail. She's so radiant and lovely. I already can't stand her.

Suddenly, Abraham addresses the group. "This is who I was telling you all about."

I blush. "You told them about me?"

"Of course. So, Dinah, these are some friends of mine. We all work together here at this restaurant."

I knew it. I am the odd one out. I try my best not to look uncomfortable.

Abraham continues, "The owner is Blended, and she knows all about this meeting."

I'm confused. "Blended, but owns a restaurant?"

"She's coded black. Not as ambiguous-looking as the rest of us. She was around when the president first started using codes. She knows what we're up to, and gives her support from a distance. Because of her, we've been able to earn a living. We just have to stay in the back."

"Except me," chimes in the black girl. "I'm one of the servers. My name is Barbara. It's nice to meet you. Dinah, right?"

"Yeah." I smile big at her, but the forced movement hurts. "Nice to meet you, too. So... you're not Blended?"

"Nope. Just black. There are brown and black people in my family, but that doesn't mean anything. Anyways, you should sit down. Get comfortable... and welcome."

Not only is this girl beautiful; She's adorable and considerate. I wonder about her and Abraham. Why are they sitting next to each other? She's a little too close for my comfort, but he doesn't seem to mind it. Does he like her? Does she like him back? I sit at the available seat at the end- between Barbara and the other couple.

"My name's Lindsay."

The brown girl on my right is warm, yet a little reserved. She's wearing a green halter top with matching dangly earrings. I'm so envious of her hair. Her curls resemble those of my wig, but they're actually growing from her scalp.

"I'm half black and half yellow, but… brown to the outside world. I don't think I've seen you before."

I shrug. "I don't know what to tell you. I'm around."

The guy sitting next to Lindsay- on her right- raises his hand.

"I'm the boyfriend…Jonathan. Half yellow, half red, but… just red, as far as the world is concerned."

The couple's dynamic boggles my mind. I assume their parents are in hiding, so now they need to be. Why complicate things by dating another illegal person? Lindsay could easily date another brown person, and Jonathan could date a red person. They could live normal lives without fear. Instead, they choose fear. I wonder how their parents feel. My parents would have been furious about me dating outside my color code.

My feelings for Abraham don't feel taboo, though. In this skin, I sometimes find myself forgetting that it isn't mine. Nobody here can say it isn't, or that a relationship between Abraham and I would be frowned upon.

"We live together," says Jonathan. "In a red-only apartment complex. No one asks any questions."

106

"Because *most* of us don't even care," says Barbara. "We spend our whole lives staying in our lanes, because Twos might be around."

The words fall out. "How do you know if someone is a Two?"

I really didn't mean to say that out loud. I'm sure that I'm already supposed to know the answer. My feelings are validated as everyone nervously laughs. I laugh back just as uncomfortably.

"I'm pretty sure a Two is responsible for what happened to Abril," says Abraham.

Jonathan scoffs. "*Or* that guy drove down here to start shit. He wouldn't be the first. Abril was probably playing on her lawn and he snatched her."

"But how'd he know about her being Blended?" asks Abraham.

"Maybe he didn't. Blended fishing is a thing."

"Blended fishing?" I blurt out under my breath.

Lindsay sighs. "We can't cross the Gate, but they're free to come through here, snatch one of us up, and turn us in."

I furrow my brows. "What if the person they take isn't actually Blended?"

"Doesn't matter." Barbara shakes her head. "That person is gone."

"Oh my. And…crossing the gate? Which gate are they using?"

Everyone turns to glare at me. It's the longest period of silence I think I've ever experienced. I look over at Abraham for reassurance, but he's just as baffled as everyone else. How badly did I just screw up?

"Hmm." Lindsay studies my face. "Maybe that's why I haven't seen you. I've lived here all of my life. 17 years. How long have you been here?"

"Long enough. I just don't know what you're talking about."

Inside, I'm groaning at my response. I can feel my heartbeat pounding inside of my chest. Coming here was a huge mistake.

"It's pretty important information," says Jonathan. "Every city has a Gate. In my hometown, it was a strip of abandoned businesses. We called it 'the haunted Gate'. Your parents never told you about any of that?"

Lindsay nods. "Here, it's that unclaimed, wooded area at the base of the hill. Stay far away from that- especially after sundown."

Wait. Is she talking about the nature preserve? Is that why it's always empty? What's wrong with it? I've never felt unsafe there. Why does sundown matter? Passing through that and their neighborhood is the only way to get downtown. I want to ask questions, so I can understand better, but I know I can't. I'm already giving off a suspicious vibe. What must Abraham think of me? Does he regret inviting me here? I feel so stupid, and that's making me upset. Am I allowed to look upset right now? My mind is so clouded. I try to relax my body and face, but everything wants to tense up.

Lindsay continues. "We do everything we're asked. We mind our business. *They* moved away from *us* decades ago, and went through all the trouble of building on that hill. You'd think they'd be happy, but that Simple Watch won't leave us alone. Now, a little girl is missing."

I'm trying my best to process everything. I've seen so much joy and freedom here, but all of them talk about their lives as if they're trapped. It doesn't match up. They have a whole town to wander through. People of multiple color codes are allowed to exist together. They can wear what they want, swim, date, and work. I haven't heard anyone talk about arranged marriages. I can't relate to their lives at all. I'm the one who is truly trapped. As for the way they talk about Simples, I'm nothing like that. I don't want to bother anyone- much less, kidnap anyone. I'm not trying to block them from areas, and I never intended to separate myself from them. It was never my choice. Nothing was. I can't be blamed for the way I was raised. I'm just as much of a victim of other Simples as they are.

Barbara breaks my concentration. "There should be more outrage. She's just a child."

"Not only that..." Jonathan jumps in. "That damn Comfort law..."

Barbara shakes her head. "Terrible."

I'm quick to roll my eyes. "You're not even Blended. None of this concerns you."

"I can't care about people?"

"I'm not saying that. You just... can't relate. No one's asking you to hide who *you* are. You don't know what it's like for us."

The group hesitates, again, to stare at me. I have no idea what's going on in their minds, but I stand by what I said. She's not illegal. No one is trying to harm her, because of what she is. She has the luxury to relax, and this doesn't have to be her fight. She spent way more time around Blended people than me, too. Did she not speak up before? What does she have to gain by speaking out now?

Barbara responds with restraint in her voice. "We don't have time to unpack how ignorant you sound. Almost everything out of your mouth... Abraham, where did you find her?"

Abraham looks at her with mild panic. I'm surprised that he's not quick to defend me. That really stings.

Jonathan speaks up instead. "We're losing focus already. We're here for Abril."

"We should organize a search party," says Abraham.

Lindsay shakes her head. "How do we look for someone with a new identity? We know she was renamed Nicole. Her code is red now. We don't have any pictures to go by. What if they totally changed her appearance, too. Knowing how she used to look might not matter."

"Good points," nods Abraham. "Shit."

"*And*," Lindsay continues. "What's our game plan if we find her? Do we look for her parents? Return her to them? There's no way we're going to be able to do all that without getting caught."

"We need to learn more about the Comfort law," Jonathan suggests. "Maybe that's our best way of finding her. We can't compromise ourselves."

Lindsay agrees. "Exposing the law will make it a lot harder for the government to hide her. It will also prevent other Blended people from falling victim to it."

"Maybe we can push to dismantle it," says Abraham with a smile.

I feel I've gone a little too long without speaking. My intellect and usefulness was already put into question, and no one is looking my way. Maybe everyone is tuning me out- including my Abe. I can't lose him. I want everyone to look at me the same way they did when I first walked into the room. Thankfully, I do have some valuable information to share with the group.

"First of all, you're never going to find her parents."

Everyone turns to face me. There are no bewildered or irritated expressions. I have their interest. I have control.

"I have a source. The reason I asked about how to know if someone is a Two... I'm pretty sure I dated one."

Lindsay's mouth is wide open. "What!?"

"And you weren't turned in?" asks Jonathan. "That can't be right."

110

I shrug my shoulders, and continue to make stuff up. "I don't think he knew I was Blended, and I never thought to mention it. He never poked around, either. He knew a lot about Simples, though, and he told me a lot about the Comfort stuff. I just never knew what to do with that information."

Abraham gives me a confused look. "Why didn't you say any of this before? Who was the guy?"

"Nevermind that mistake." I shake my head. "Besides, he won't help us. He just wanted to brag. You want to know what I know or not?"

Everyone glances at each other before putting their focus back onto me. I really want to smile as I carry on.

"When someone is turned in, that person isn't the only one who disappears. The proof does, too. Abril's parents are proof that she existed. Wherever that little girl is now, she has a new family, and not even that new family has any idea of who she used to be."

"How is that possible?" asked Barbara. "She didn't fall out of thin air."

"We're talking about the government. They have resources. My ex told me they'll even make up whole adoption agencies and sob stories to get a family interested. You'll have a whole new name, code, and physical features. They never want you found. They might even send you to an entirely different state."

"Would they really send April that far?" asks Lindsay.

"They'll do whatever they feel they need to," says Jonathan. "So... Are we going to assume her parents are dead?"

I nod. "Abril... or Nicole... is still alive, though... As long as she follows the rules."

Lindsay's eyes widen. "What do you mean?"

"Her life will be spared, as long as she agrees to live the rest of her life as a red-coded girl with her new family. If she brings any attention to the truth, they will get rid of her."

"She's a 5 year-old girl," says Barbara. "She won't understand any of that. This is really a race against time then. As soon as she acts out, she's gone. Like... *really* gone, because not even the news is talking about this."

Abraham sighs. "So... We're looking for a girl named Abril who can only respond to Nicole. We don't know what she used to look like, and we don't know what she looks like now. We don't know where she is, or who she's with. The only sources we have on the Comfort law are a member of the Simple Watch, and a possible Two. And her parents might be dead."

I watch as Barbara rubs Abraham's arm, then rests her head on it. So *that's* why she wants to be here. She's not interested in the missing girl. She wants time with Abraham. She's so pathetic. He hardly looks at her. Sure, I'm here for him too, and he's hardly looking at me. At least, I don't look desperate. At least, I have something to add to the conversation, because- unlike her- I belong here.

"You're right, Johnny." Lindsay scoots her chair closer to her boyfriend, and puts her arms around him. "We need to blow the lid off Comfort for Community. It's the only way to find her."

Then, she turns to me. "So grateful you're here, Dinah. That ex of yours served a purpose after all. I wonder if anyone else in the Lowlands has information."

Jonathan gently kisses his girlfriend on the forehead. "We should send feelers out."

I find his and Lindsay's affection fascinating. I never witnessed it at either of my homes or neighborhoods. It's seen as rude or distracting. Here, it's so open and expected. You don't need to be married, either. Maybe that's why I'm so eager to be affectionate with Abraham. It's a part of the culture. I'm adapting to it so quickly.

As much as I tried to be a good Simple, I just couldn't. It never clicked. I was never happy. Here, I feel safe and heard. I feel important. Maybe the same rules apply for the Blended. I'm happy and fulfilled as one, so I must be one.

"Should we name ourselves?" asks Barabara. "I mean, to sound more established?"

Lindsay still has her arms around Jonathan. "The Blended works for me. Let's keep the name, but change how people perceive us."

"That's not gonna happen," says Abraham. "Not in our lifetime."

Barbara adds, "What if people who *aren't* Blended want to join in? Like me? If y'all get arrested just for revealing yourselves, the cause is over. We need numbers, and people at all fronts."

"Hmm." says Lindsay. "How about we call ourselves The Bowl? Think about it: We're blended like smoothies, but…smoothies start out as individual fruits…or other ingredients. Some of those ingredients start out in a bowl. They have their own uniqueness, but can coexist together. It brings attention to what that smoothie was before, and has always been. Plus, people on the outside will have no idea what we're talking about. We won't set off any alarms. I mean, we could have a really cool name, or one that defines us better…or we could have a name so ridiculous, no one sees us coming."

Abraham shakes his head. "I don't want to sound ridiculous or muddle the message, and I don't want any more fruit or smoothie analogies. That shit never sat well with me. That Comfort for Community law? That makes *them* comfortable. We should be comfortable telling our truth. They should listen, and they should care. *We* are uncomfortable. We're.. .the Discomfort."

The energy of the group lit up, as we nodded in unison. Abe is brilliant. He has me so impressed, I forgot to be very worried about all of this. Exposing Comfort for Community will end my protection, and expose my Simple background to the group. Even worse, I could be killed in order for the government to hide their tracks. I want to impress Abraham, but I can't let these people actually succeed.

16

"I choose to change."

As we all step out of the restaurant, a full moon is on display. Something about it feels serendipitous. Lindsay and Jonathan wave goodbye, then walk to their car. I make sure to pull Abraham aside before Barbara gets a chance to. I know she's thinking about it, trailing close behind him.

I dramatically gasp and lean in. "Hey, Abe. I could raise a lot of money for the cause by selling… Well, you know."

He gives me a surprisingly troubled look, then turns to address Barbara. "Be safe getting home."

She reacts a little off guard. "Thanks. You, too."

"I will. See you tomorrow. I just need to tell Dinah something before heading home myself. I'm exhausted."

"I understand," she says. "You had a long day. Nice meeting you, Dinah."

I hardly look in her direction. "You, too."

Finally, she leaves us alone.

Abraham sighs. "Yeah, about that… That's gonna be a problem. Might make more sense to toss whatever you have left."

"That doesn't make any sense at all. I can make a lot of money off that stuff. No one has to know where it came from... just where it's going."

"The best thing you can do is distance yourself from that. I haven't told any of them about it, and I don't plan to. I was wrong to buy off of you."

"But if you didn't, we never would have met." I smile.

Abraham doesn't smile back. "I stopped using the stuff. Never gave it a chance to do its thing. Dinah, if we're going to lead, we need to lead by example. Illegally profiting off of government-level skin bleach sends the wrong message."

I hear words coming out, but I don't understand. He makes the whole thing sound dirty. Throwing the bleach away would be wasteful, and harmful to the environment. It's also the equivalent of setting hundreds of dollars on fire. What I do is provide a service. No one has to give up their personal information, so my service is safer than the alternative. The message is survival. He can't benefit from my products on multiple occasions, just to turn around and say they're bad.

I cross my arms. "It happened, though."

"You're right. I choose to change."

"I want change, too."

"Then you know what to do. See you later." With that, he walks away.

I love Abraham, but he doesn't see the big picture. He has the privilege of being able to support himself. I bet he got to choose his job. Selling Enlightenment is my only option. I have every intention of sharing my wealth and journey with him. He'd be missing out, if I stopped. One day, he'll understand, and he'll be grateful. I'm not going to stop selling. Besides, it's better that we profit privately, than pass on the wealth to the group. He did me a favor by saying 'no'.

Walking back to the car, Barbara seemingly comes out of nowhere.

"Hey, Dinah."

"Hey."

"I walked all the way to my car, but something is still eating at me. I know everyone else wanted to move on, but... What you said really bothered me. We don't have to be best friends, but I'm not the enemy. I want everyone to belong... to feel safe. That's why we're all here. We all want the same thing for each other."

"Abraham has nothing to do with it?"

"You think I'm here for a man? I'm here, because I can relate. Yeah, I get to be visible, but I'm *too* visible. My anger stands out. My failures stand out. When I walk into a store, I stand out. My skin stands out. I'd love to be invisible... to not be under a microscope all the time. And yeah, none of this code stuff affects me or my family. We never stopped being black. We never stopped being treated as lesser than. Those same segregation laws my people fought so hard against came back. The president says he wants things to be Simple. Easy for him to say, because he set the standard. Those who already fit the standard have nothing to worry about. What about the rest of us?"

I scoff. "Simple women don't fit the standard, either. They're servants in their own homes, and they don't even get to pick their homes. They can't wear their hair down, or express themselves through their clothes. They can't date or swim like you can."

Barbara laughs. That sets me off.

"It's not funny. Simple women are forced into servitude, and expected to be grateful. They can't speak up. They can't be trusted. You don't know how suffocating it is to be born into a role that you never agreed on, but you're not allowed to be anything else. You're not here because you have to be. You want to be. Being where *I* want to be... is a privilege I'd love to have."

Barbara pauses. Her facial expression gradually moves from puzzled to mildly disgusted. "Interesting."

"What?"

"It's just... You know a lot about... what might have happened to Abril."

"I told you. All that info came from my ex."

"Did it?"

We stare each other down for a long minute. All I can hear is my breathing, and I can't sense anything else around me.

She nods. "So... it's way past sundown. I'd warn you to stay far away from the Gate, but I don't think anyone will mess with you there."

She throws a peace sign at me, then walks away. This is not good.

***

As soon as I get into my car, I take advantage of the seclusion and darkness by carefully washing off my makeup. I constantly scan the area as I do so, and decide to keep my wig on. No one is around, and all I hear is wind, but I'm still on edge.

Driving through the nature preserve- I mean, the Gate- is surreal. The darkness accentuates the glow of flashlights moving about the trees. I think I saw four, but I wasn't paying that much attention. Getting closer to the house, I remember to throw off my wig, and stuff it into my purse.

Like clockwork, as soon as I approach the door, it opens. It's the man. His wife is seated on the couch. Both of them look exhausted and worried.

"Good evening, Sir and Ma'am. I'm sorry to keep you waiting for so long."

The man shakes his head. "How did it go?"

The woman walks me over to the couch to sit down. Her husband seats himself on the armchair across from us.

I breathe in deeply, then exhale. "Very successful. We know exactly who the ringleader is."

17

"Before meeting you, I thought Twos were some kind of boogeyman."

The man told me the situation will be handled. He didn't elaborate, but that's fine. It's not for me to think about anymore, so I don't bother.

I'm getting ready for another fake Simple Watch meeting, and neither of the Clarks are hesitating to let me go. It's an incredible feeling. It's almost as if I'm an equal in the household. We have actual conversations. I do housework like a woman, and have responsibilities outside the home like a man.

The woman is still allowing me to call her 'Mom' whenever her husband isn't around. I do it, but remind myself not to get too comfortable. Life with the couple is tolerable, but my relationship with them won't matter at all once I'm married. It will be all about my husband, and I still have no idea who that will be.

***

Out of morbid curiosity, I stop by the Soul Code Kitchen unannounced. I don't see Barbara anywhere. Abraham isn't here, either. I'm directed by a brown woman- I assume, the owner- to the kitchen. Lindsay is washing dishes, and Jonathan is cooking. They see me, and immediately panic. Lindsay stops doing the dishes, then rushes over to me.

"You must have heard. Abraham called you?"

"Of course."

He didn't, and I'm offended by that. I already have an idea of what Linday's talking about anyway. I wonder why he didn't reach out to me. I can't ask any questions, though. Information needs to be fed to me.

Lindsay holds onto my arm as if she's trying to hold herself up. She's as distraught as I am impatient.

"We called her a few times, but no response. Then... we checked the cameras."

"You got it on camera?"

"Well... kinda. Turns out she did show up for her shift. She just never came inside. Some guy walked up to her as soon as she got out of her car. They talked for a bit. Then both got into her car and drove off."

"Did you get a good look at the guy?"

"Not really. The biggest thing that stood out was his dark green hoodie."

I let out a small gasp. I have an idea. "Dark green hoodie?"

"Yeah. Why?"

"Maybe I'm overthinking, but... that reminds me of my ex. He had a favorite hoodie that was dark green. Wore it all the time."

"The Two?"

"Why would she run off with a Two?" Jonathan is listening in on our conversation, as busy as he is. Good.

"We've already been compromised," says Lindsay. "You know... Before meeting you, I thought Twos were some kind of

121

boogeyman. 'You better behave, or else the Twos will get you.' Maybe they really are out there to get us."

She lets go of my arms, and looks away. After a moment of thinking to herself, she looks back at me.

"That ex… What is his name?"

"His name? Oh… Richard. The bastard's name is Richard. Hey, do you think they're working together?"

"Barbara with him? Not at all. She wouldn't do something like that. No. Something is very wrong."

"Maybe you guys don't know her as well as you thought. Not everyone is who they present themselves to be. I'm sure exposing our group would be very lucrative."

I can feel the sweat on my skin. If I stay here in the kitchen too long, my makeup will smear. My scalp underneath the wig is starting to feel a little itchy, too.

Lindsay shakes her head. "No. Barbara isn't like that. I've known her for years. She's the sweetest, most dependable person ever. She wouldn't sell us out, and she's not the type to leave without saying something."

"Okay, but the whole thing looks very suspicious to me. Look, I need to go. I'll see you at the next meeting."

I leave in such a rush, I forget to acknowledge Jonathan. I get into my car, lock it, then check on my makeup. Turns out I just need a little touch up. That's something I can realistically do out in the open. I pull out some foundation from my purse and get to work.

Part of me wants to sit and analyze what happened to Barbara, but there's no need to put my mind there. I did what I did out of necessity. I didn't want to harm her, and that's why I didn't. My hands are clean. She was going to expose me. My life was in danger. She'd do the same in my position. It was a fair fight. I was just quicker. I had no choice, but to use the cards that society dealt me. I'm not a bad person. It's the world that's harsh. It breeds desperation. I know she and the rest of the group want to change the rules. In the meantime, we only have what we're given. I had no choice.

I start up the engine, and head to the pool.

18

"Does that mean I can't stop?"

I'm scanning the crowd for Abraham as I head to the restroom with my purse full of goodies. Thankfully, he's not here. It feels strange to *not* want him around. It's for his own good, though. I step inside the restroom.

"Hey, there."

It's Amanda, my first customer. In a short time, we've come a long way from her being suspicious of me. Now the teen tells me all kinds of details about her day and life. I usually zone out, because I'm more concerned about seeing Abraham. Amanda is also not as brown as she used to be. I'd hardly code her as white, though. Her lighter skin only accentuates the darkness of her hair and eyes, as well as the broadness of her nose. She hardly looks human, but she seems happy.

"Hi, Amanda. How are you?"

"Good." She looks down at my purse.

"Okay, so... I do have something for you. Come to my car?"

"Your car?"

"Yep."

Without another word, I calmly walk back to the parking lot. I can feel Amanda's presence close behind me. I'm confident that she will follow me anywhere, and hold onto anything I tell her. She won't fight me, because she needs me. It feels nice to be held in such high regard.

I unlock my car with the key fob, then sit in the driver's seat. Amanda sits in the front passenger seat. I can feel her eagerness for me to say something, so I take my time. It feels like waving a piece of food in front of a hungry dog who knows better than to lunge. It just sits and stares, waiting patiently for you to let go. As far as anyone on the outside is concerned, nothing out of the ordinary is happening.

"Amanda… I'm not selling anymore."

"Wait. What? Why?"

"Change of plans. A movement is rising. You won't need those creams anymore."

"What are you talking about? Does this have anything to do with Abril?"

"Yes. Can I trust you with something?"

Amanda grins. "Of course."

"Okay. So… I'm part of a group calling itself The Discomfort. We plan on totally dismantling Comfort for Community."

"Holy shit," whispers Amanda. Her eyes are so big, they might fall out of her head. "How?"

"So much is brewing, but… Here's the part that concerns you the most right now: The group doesn't want me to sell anymore skin bleach. You understand why, right?"

"Sure, but… do you have any Enlightenment on you now?"

I exaggerate a sigh. I want her to think I'm so bummed out about the whole fake ordeal.

"I do, and that's the problem. My source is pushing for me to sell. I'm not sure how to get out of it, and I can't give the tubs away."

"Who is your source?"

"You know I can't tell you that, but if I don't sell..." Another sigh. "Anyways, that's nothing for you to worry about. I'll figure something out. I just wanted you to know."

I look down at my feet and stay quiet. My mind travels to Abraham holding me close under the shade of our oak tree. I can smell and feel his rough skin, and hear his heart beating. No one else is around for miles. I close my eyes. The vision feels so real.

"Maybe... you don't have to sell," says Amanda. The sound of her voice snaps me back into reality. I'm so annoyed, but my energy must go into pretending not to know what she's alluding to. She's the one who needs to say it out loud.

"I can't give them away, Amanda. I already told you that."

"I know. I mean... Maybe I can help. Maybe if I knew your source, they can send the stuff to me, and..."

"Impossible. The deal is that *I* sell, and I can't let anyone else know about them. You can't help me." I try my best to tear up, but it just isn't happening.

"What if they send the creams to you, and then you give them to me... to sell? Would they know?"

"I don't know, but... that's a big responsibility. All of the products would need to be sold. You couldn't be a dollar short."

Amanda gives it some thought, but I can't allow her to think too hard.

I interrupt her. "There's a lot of money in it, though. I gotta admit: the money is nice."

I pull out my purse. I knew my words and sympathetic eyes would only get me so far with Amanda. I need to seal the deal. As soon as I pull a wad of cash out of my wallet, the teen fully stops concentrating on whatever it was.

"This is one grand. Want to hold it?"

Amanda's face lights up.

"You can have it."

"Wait... what?"

"Take the money. You have the potential to earn so much more. You're familiar with the product. You know its quality... its worth. You're familiar with this location, and there's already a built-in client list. You won't have any trouble. There are just a couple of rules you need to follow."

"Sure. What are they?"

"I'm going to give you all the products I have on me. My source gives me 48 hours to come up with the money."

"Okay. How much money will you need?"

"At least, as much as I handed you. That money belongs to them- not me. That grand becomes yours, *if* you can make up the difference. Should be easy to do."

"Okay. Um... You normally charge $100. How many creams do you have?"

"One dozen."

Amanda did the math in her head. "I'll get to keep $200 if I sell at that price."

I smirk. "That's not bad."

Amanda pauses. "But if I charge more, then I can keep more?"

"Exactly. A grand goes to my source, as they need proof of sale. You get to keep the rest. And, hey... if you decide this isn't for you, then you're free to walk away after the job is done. No pressure. I'll never tell anyone."

Amanda smiles, but I can feel her hesitation as much as I can feel her trying to psych herself up. I know she doesn't want to let me down. I didn't even need to lock the car or threaten her. She followed me. She got into the car with me. She's listening to me, and intends to do what I told her to do. She reminds me a lot of my old self, as I used to be just as willing and obedient.

"Are you ready, Amanda?"

"Yes."

"Good. I'll give you my whole bag. I'll be back in this spot in 48 hours to collect the money. If you decide to run off with the money and product, they will come looking for you. They will kill you, but not before torturing you first. I care about you too much to let that happen. Please be careful, Amanda. Best to do what you're told, then you can keep all that money and leave with no issues."

Amanda gives me a thumbs up. "Okay. I can do that."

"I know you can. Thank you for helping me."

I give her a hug, as something else to leave her with. I want the last thing for her to remember is my touch, rather than the money and danger. I remember my husband's touch. He was really attentive and kind in the beginning. I never loved him. I was never even attracted to him. I'm not sure why I'm even thinking of all this now. I'm kind of surprised by how receptive Amanda is to my touch. She's hugging me tighter than I am her.

I give her the bag, and she gets out of the car. I had already stashed my makeup, water bottle and washcloth in the glove compartment with the gun. My wallet is in my hand. I start up the car and drive off. In my rearview mirror, I can see Amanda walking back to the restroom with my stash. I know she's going to do well.

***

2 days later, I stop by the pool restroom. It's becoming a lot easier to leave the house, now that my new parents- Jaxtyn and Quinn- think I'm doing great things for the community. I'm even bothering to remember their names now. They haven't brought up

any sort of suitor, but that doesn't mean they don't have one lined up. I don't plan on staying with them much longer anyway.

I see Amanda waiting for me with my bag as soon as I pull into the lot. She has a goofy smile on her face. I smile back. It feels good to know someone is happy to see me. I guess Quinn is happy to see me sometimes, but I don't want to feel thrilled to see her back. I don't particularly care for Amanda, either. I can't care about her, but I do need her.

I park the car, and signal at Amanda to get into the passenger seat. She does as instructed.

I present my happiest expression. "How did it go?"

"Crazy how I could tell who to talk to. They always looked lost, like they were waiting for you. I made up some story about supplies being low, so I had to jack up the price. They actually paid it."

"And?" I wasn't asking about her experience.

"$2400... Which means I can keep the money you gave me!"

"Great work!" I held my hand out.

Amanda hands me all of the cash. She glows as I count and give her $1000. I'm sure I was glowing, too. I put the rest of the money in my wallet, then put the wallet into my purse.

"I'm so proud of you, Amanda. I hope you enjoy the fruits of your labor."

"Thank you, Dinah!"

"I do have some bad news, though."

The smile on the teen's face quickly fades. "Bad news?"

"Somehow word got back that you were selling. My source knows all about you. After your performance today, they're going to want to keep you around. Did you talk to anyone who seemed off? Anything look weird to you?"

"Not at all. Everything was so smooth. Too smooth."

"Hmm... Maybe that's the problem. Maybe the area is being watched. I had no idea, Amanda. I'm so sorry. I didn't mean to involve you like this."

"Wait. Does that mean I can't stop?"

I try my best to look worried, and unable to look her in the eye. "You know too much, and you're handling their money. Give me time to think of something, but yeah... You are now expected to sell."

All of the color leaves Amanda's face. "What if I stop coming to the pool? Can I just disappear? I won't say anything."

"Doesn't matter."

"Are we being watched right now?"

I lie. "I see someone in the corner of my eye just standing there, watching us. Someone I've never seen before." Amanda begins to panic. "Stay calm. We know what needs to be done. As long as the product moves, and they make a profit, everything is fine. Like I said, give me time to figure something out. In the meantime, we need to protect each other."

"How?"

"We'll keep each other a secret. We already know the consumers will keep their mouths shut, because of their need for the supply. Think of your knowledge of me as insurance. If you go down, you can take me with you. You might be able to save yourself."

Amanda shakes her head. "I won't say anything. I promise."

"You also need to keep the source happy. Money has to keep rolling in, but you only need to worry about that at the beginning of each month. Keep my purse. I'll come by with the stuff, and give you 48 hours to sell. Same as before."

"And I still need to sell over $1000?"

"You need to sell as much as you want to bring home. Now, they're going to expect- at least- $2000, but that can change… and on a whim. I don't make the rules. The more you earn, the more you can take home. So keep that in mind."

Things get quiet. I know Amanda wants to say something, but- for the first time- she's holding back. It reminds me of dealing with my mother. Like Amanda, I was mouthy when I was younger. My mother was quick to make me feel guilty for being that way. Simplicity for a young girl meant playing nice. That meant keeping my mouth shut. Performance was more important than reality. Being quiet made me look calm and impressionable. In reality, my silence was loud. I groan, but Amanda's rambling lets me know exactly what's going on inside of her mind, and what she's capable of. In order to keep that up, I can never let her feel as if she can't talk to me.

"What is it, honey?"

"Since I'm in it, can you tell me what the source is?"

I shake my head. "I'm trying to get you out, though. With that knowledge, you'll never escape this. Trust me. Meanwhile, you do have the potential to make a lot of money."

Amanda bursts into tears. That wasn't the reaction I expected at all. My shoulders are tensing up, and I have no idea what to do with my body. I'm knee deep in this now, though. I can't back out, and I can't let her. All I know is the same basic thing I was told every time I cried. Specifically, every time I cried, *and* wasn't completely ignored. I numbly embrace her, and say:

"Oh, Amanda. This crying…I know it feels like relief. It isn't. You and I were brought together for a reason. You are proving your worth. Instead of being grateful for the opportunity, you are pitying yourself, because the road is hard. Well, the tougher the road, the more worthy the award. Tears will mess with your endurance and focus. You're not on your own, either. I am with you. I am right here with you. There's no need to worry, because I already carry that worry for you. I will see to it that everything works out. So when you cry, you are saying that you don't trust my care for you. Do you trust me?"

The teen sniffles, still in my arms. "I do."

"Thank you, Amanda. Thank you."

She sniffles some more, then backs away to wipe her tears. She looks at me, doing her best to curl the ends of her lips and brighten her eyes. I can still see the pain. Did anyone ever see mine when I was her age? In this position, I always thought I'd be more attentive. I'd do all I could to listen to my daughter, and support the path she wanted for herself. Now, I see that I'm no better. I don't need Amanda's silence in the way my mother needed mine. I just need her to perform her role, as proof of how influential my performance is. After all, love and concern is expressed through duty.

19

"We can not and will not tolerate organizing against us."

Another morning.

I wake up, put on my clothes, and meet Quinn in the kitchen. She happily greets me with a little hug. Something about her hugs make me feel as if I'm being pulled downward. I fight the urge to push her off.

"Good morning, honey. I hope you slept well."

"I did. Thank you, Mom."

"Good. Okay, let's get to work."

We prepare eggs, bacon, waffles, and sausage. I still need to hold back my groans while cooking, because it feels like a big waste of time. I don't recall the president ever telling women to make enormous meals, but it's normal to fill the table with food and decor.

It's also normal to give husbands the lion's share of the food. Eating anything he leaves on his plate is considered stealing, so it's thrown away. Whatever the wives and children don't finish on their plates must also be thrown out. I know that holding onto leftovers was more acceptable when my parents were younger. These days, Simples see leftovers as a sign of a man's inability to provide financially. All meals must be fresh.

Seeing Quinn's cheerful face irritates me. She's really enjoying all of this. She doesn't want anything beyond this. Even calling her 'Mom' physically hurts. I have to force myself to do it. I can't upset her illusion, because then I'd have to deal with the repercussions of that. At least, this current version of her lets me leave the house more often.

***

Jaxtyn finishes his breakfast and leaves. Quinn and I eat our share, then cleaned the kitchen together. Quinn is now cleaning the bathroom, while I'm cleaning the living room. I've already dusted. Now, I'm disinfecting. After that, I plan to vacuum. I'm so lost in the trance of my movements. I hardly notice Quinn coming up behind me.

"Let's take a break?"

"Oh. Okay, Mom."

"Come with me back to the kitchen."

I follow behind her. It bothers me more and more to do that. She sits at the table, and motions for me to sit on the chair next to her. She smiles, and I mechanically smile back.

"How have you been, Dinah?"

I don't know how to respond to that. I'm irritated that she disrupted my work to ask me such a thing. What's going on in her mind? Is she suspecting something? Is she trying to get me to confess something? Just in case, I'm going to keep my responses down to a minimum.

She sighs. "It's just that... So many serious things happened in a short period of time. We were so caught up in how to handle them, I never checked in on you. Not as well as I should have. You've been with the Simple Watch a lot lately, and you're making great strides in keeping the Highlands safe. I want you to know that I'm thinking of you, and I'm proud of you."

"Thank you, Mom."

"I have great news as well. Your father has been very impressed by you, too. He's been keeping his eyes open, and having some fruitful conversations. He wanted me to be the one to tell you. There's much to prepare for."

Oh, no. Not now. Please, not now.

Quinn grins.

"He found you a suitor, honey. A revolution is absolutely happening. You have been so courageous and diligent. It's only fitting that you are paired with a soldier. He's a member of the all-male Simple Watch. Your father went to a meeting to pass along your information. I was pleased to hear that none of them ever heard of you. Proves you really have been obedient while out and about. Only loose women make impressions. Anyways, as soon as you told us about that black, your suitor was the one trusted to spring into action. After all, *he* was the one to expose that lawbreaking family."

I can feel my eyes widen. "He took Abril?"

"Or whatever her name is now. And he didn't *take* her. He rescued an abused girl, and took the necessary steps to ensure she'd grow up in a law-abiding, stable home. He's a hero. People in the Lowlands are outraged, because we don't allow them to upset the foundation of this nation. We have a right to be comfortable. They even started a terrorist group called The Discomfort, because they know exactly how they harm us."

I think my heart stopped for a moment. "The Discomfort?"

"Your future husband went back to that same restaurant last night. Those idiots had a window open, and he heard everything. He set the whole place on fire."

I can't feel my body anymore. My eyes are open, but my vision is blurry. I'm sure my face reads how upset I am, but I don't have the energy to collect myself.

"Were... were they inside?"

"I'm sure he waited until they left. We Simples have some sense. He just wanted to send a message. It's all about survival. We can not and will not tolerate organizing against us. After all, we are the true Americans. Your work has been invaluable, honey. Your husband can continue fighting for the Greater Good, while you stay dutifully at home."

"But, I don't.. I mean, is... What happened to Barbara?"

"She can't disrupt us anymore. No more *discomfort*. None of that has anything to do with us anyway. Our hands are clean."

Suddenly, Quinn lights up. "Oh, I forgot! Your husband... David... I can't say enough wonderful things about him. He is an exceptional leader, and you'll benefit greatly from his wisdom. I am so excited for you, honey. So, his 40th birthday is next month. We want to present your marriage to him as a gift. Your father and I are arranging everything, so you can relax. After everything you've been through, he's the perfect man to keep you on the Simple path. He's also eager for children."

"David?" That's all I could push out of my mouth.

"Yes, honey. I'm going to miss you very much. It has been lovely having you here, but I know you'll be in good hands. Let's get back to work, yes?"

"Yes, Mom."

I can't face her, but I can feel her smiling eyes on me. I get up and return to disinfecting the living room furniture. Before, I was lost in the rhythm of my movements. Now, my limbs are numb.

I'm not angry or sad; I'm not sure how else to be. As much as I tried to not get attached to the Clarks, I realize that I am. I guess part of me thought Quinn would be different somehow. She wants me around, but she needs to please her husband. Her love is expressed by making me as dutiful to him. Soon, I'll be dutiful to another man. I can't let that happen. I can't undo all that I have done to get to this point, and after all I have witnessed in the Lowlands. There is something better out there. I can be better. My hands can't be clean anymore.

20

"That was a really cool, brave, and kinda stupid thing you just did."

I'm taking full advantage of the time I have left to go to my fake Simple Watch meetings. I'm so grateful for how willfully ignorant Quinn is. Since she doesn't socialize with anyone outside of the household, it has been extremely easy to lie. There's no one to verify that I've been going to meetings, and no one to verify that I haven't. The funny thing is if I expressed interest in meeting up with friends that she knew about, there would be way more scrutiny. Quinn would drive me to and from, and Jaxtyn would ask all kinds of questions.

I texted Abraham earlier, asking him to meet me at the oak tree. Our oak tree. I told him it was about Barbara. He didn't hesitate to set up a time. I'm glad, because I really miss him.

I arrive at the pool parking lot. He's already here- waiting for me, and fidgeting on his phone. My eyes travel over his broad shoulders, and his lean, long body. I can already smell him, and my stomach is filling up with butterflies. I step out of the car, and walk towards him in what feels like slow motion. As I move in closer, he looks up and gives me a half smile.

"Hey, Dinah."

"Oh, Abe." I give him a hug, making sure to press firmly against his body while I have the chance. "I'm so glad you're okay."

"Where have you been?"

His cold energy is throwing me off. I thought he'd be happier to see me. "Tied up with things at home. I know we're trying to be discreet, but every single one of you has been on my mind. How are Lindsay and Jonathan?"

"Shaken up, but alive. Our boss is heartbroken, though."

"That's devastating. I'm so sorry, Abe. How are you holding up?"

"I'm fine. You know who did it?"

What does he mean by that? "No."

"You don't think your ex was involved? Didn't he kidnap Barbara?"

I shake my head. "I told Lindsay that *maybe* he did, but I don't know for sure. I think Barbara knew whoever it was that day, and left willingly. Why else would she let him in her car? How did he know that she worked at the Soul Code Cafe? He learned through her. Maybe it was *her* crazy ex."

"But why would he set her job on fire?"

I shrug my shoulders. "I don't know. The person she drove off with and the person who started the fire could be totally different people."

"Maybe *another* crazy ex is involved?"

I can't hold back an eye roll. "I don't know, Abe."

"Well, I think the kidnapping and fire are related."

"It's possible, but… I really don't think Barbara was kidnapped. We have to look into her schedule… her social circles.

The Simple Watch learned all about The Discomfort from someone. The cafe was burned down in retaliation."

"Wait a minute. How do you know that? I'm confused. You don't know who is guilty, but you know enough that Simples are behind this? Who told you that?"

Oh, I really messed up. There hasn't been much of a need to keep my stories straight with Quinn and Jaxtyn. I underestimated Abraham. Honestly, I never saw him being this invested. I have to come up with an excuse quickly.

"No one did. I... It just makes a whole lot of sense. Like, I said... She wasn't kidnapped, but I bet she needed it to look that way. A missing person can't be a guilty person. The people who knew her had all the facts... Where she could be found, and the significance of the cafe. Why burn it down? To scare us. They're not worried about coffee or pastries. They knew we were plotting something. Maybe they didn't know about The Discomfort, in name, specifically. What they did know was because of Barbara. She was a Two."

Abraham shakes his head and laughs. "She's not Blended."

"But she spent time around Blended people, and wanted to be involved with the movement. Said she cares about others, but- "

"She does, though. She's really sweet and dependable. I've known her for years. She would never turn on us like that. You need to get a hold of your ex, and find out what's going on. If he's as arrogant as you said he is, he's probably dying to brag about all he knows."

I can feel my mouth hang open. I'm surprised none of that worked. I try my best to conceal how flustered I am.

"But... I deleted his number."

"You don't know where to find him? No mutual friends?"

"Look... even if I could find him, I'd be compromising myself."

Abraham rolls his eyes. "So... 'do nothing' is the solution?"

"I'm not saying that. I care about Barbara."

"Even though you think she's a Two?"

"I want to know what's going on as much as everyone else, Abe. We just need to be careful. We need witnesses, in case something happens to us. We could also benefit from better awareness and growth of the group."

Words are just falling out of my mouth as I scramble to think of an explanation he'll accept. Only one more idea comes to mind.

"Maybe... We can get on social media."

Abraham raises an eyebrow. "You think that's a *careful* solution?"

"I have a burner phone, and I can use fake info. We can get the word out about Barbara and Abril. Our movement could grow so big, no one could ignore us... or even threaten us without the world watching. Simples and Twos would tread lightly, not wanting to incriminate themselves."

I instantly feel the tension in my upper body release as he nods.

He asks, "How soon do you wanna do that?"

"How about right now? Give me a sec."

I pull out my phone, upload the app, and sign up for an account. It's surprisingly easy enough. I've never been allowed on social media. It's seen as a vain distraction. However, Simples in positions of power are allowed to have accounts. In a way, I'm recognized as being in a position of power. So, maybe I'm not breaking any rules. I honestly don't know why I even care in the first place. In the long run, I want nothing to do with Simplicity.

I name our account *The_Discomfort*. For the profile picture, I take an upward photo from beneath our sacred oak tree. For the profile caption, I type: A voice for the Blended.

I hand the phone over to Abraham. He approves of what he sees.

"This is great. Why this tree, though?"

"It's... vague, but it holds a lot of meaning."

"Like the growth of a tree moving upward and providing for others? Like food, shade and stuff? Mutually beneficial and long-lasting, and all that?"

"Sure. Basically."

"Cool. Let's start posting."

"About what?"

I'm so wrapped up in the thrill of being on social media, I totally forgot about why I suggested it. That clearly upsets Abraham.

"What the hell, Dinah?"

That's right. Barbara and Abril. I really need to redeem myself, before Abraham gets too suspicious. He's looking at me the same way Barbara did.

"I have an idea. I'll post a live video, then upload when done."

"Right now?"

"We can't wait another minute, right?"

I sit down and clear my throat. Abraham sits down next to me. We both look around to see if anyone is paying attention. It's not crowded, and no one is looking. It feels like such a sweet, in-sync moment between us. I have all of his attention right now. I need to make it worth his while. I point the camera toward me and begin recording.

"Hi, everyone. This is Gertrude with The Discomfort- a community of Blended people about to change the country. People like me can't exist, but we do exist. One of our founding members has gone missing, here in the state of North California. Her name is Barbara, and we believe she was kidnapped. She was seen, on video, driving away with a mystery man. That man may have been a Two. That Two may also have information behind her place of employment being burned down. There have been no arrests or leads. If you know what I'm talking about, and have any information, please message us. We will keep your information safe. We need to find her, because her life may be in danger. There are people who want to stop what we're doing before we even start."

I look at Abraham, who is off-camera. He's looking at me with such bewilderment and joy. His positive reaction energizes me to keep going.

"Also... We are looking for a 5 year-old Blended girl named Abril. She might respond to the name, Nicole. She was kidnapped from her home- also here in North California- by a Simple. That Simple's name is David, and he's a member of the Simple Watch. He kidnapped Abril, and utilized the Comfort for Community program. That program is not what you think it is. She was moved to a mystery location. Her name and color codes were also changed. Plus, her parents- an interracial couple- are now missing. We need to find them, find Abril, and find Barbara. We, The Discomfort, will not rest until they are found, and people are made accountable for their crimes."

I stop recording, then upload the video on my profile. I deeply exhale, and look back at Abraham. His mouth is wide open.

"Holy shit," he says under his breath. I giggle. Then, he asks, "You know who kidnapped Abril? And why are you calling yourself Gertrude?"

I could feel all of the color leave my body. "I- ."

"How long have you known? Why didn't you say anything before? Another wild suspicion of yours?"

I give the best explanation I can come up with. "Well... People talk, right? That's the same way you found out about Abril in the first place. I only found out about David super recently, and it was by overhearing two other people in the neighborhood. I figured you, of all people, knew already. That's why you talked more about Barbara. We have less information on her. I'm sorry for assuming, though. I'll make sure to run info by you before recording again. I didn't mean to stress you out."

"That's my first time hearing his name."

"Again, I'm sorry."

"You don't need to be. So... why Gertrude?"

I didn't notice me using my birth name before he said anything. I'm horrified with myself, but my mistake may work in my favor.

"Well... I'll use my face, but I don't want to use my actual name. I need to give people some kind of identifier. For connection, you know."

Abraham nods. "Okay, Gertrude. Hmm. You know... I might just call you that from now on."

"I wouldn't mind it."

He smiles. "That was a really cool, brave, and kinda stupid thing you just did."

"Thanks, Abe."

I rub his arm, then lean my cheek against it. He bends his head down to give me a gentle kiss. We turn our bodies towards each other, and the kiss becomes deeper. When I breathe in, I ingest his aroma, and every part of me tingles. Nothing outside of us exists. We might as well be floating in midair, his strong arms cradling me. The excitement of this moment leaves me breathless, and I have to release myself from his embrace for air.

I gaze into his eyes. "Was that a mistake, too?"

"I don't think it ever was, Gertrude."

He kisses me again. This time, he slowly moves his hand up towards my wig. I can tell he wants to move his fingers through, but I can't let him. I pull away.

"Don't."

"Wh-what happened?"

"This is moving too fast for me. I need more time."

"Okay… Okay. I respect that."

"Thank you. I better go. I'll post more soon. You should follow me, and have Lindsay and Jonathan follow me, too. That darn algorithm, right? Gotta feed it."

Abraham looks dumbfounded. "Yeah."

This hurts. I really want more of him, but I can't. I don't know why I never thought of any of this before. He can't see my body or my real hair. I love him calling me by my real name, though. It's almost as if he prefers it, because he knows the truth. I'm convinced that we've been connected on a spiritual level since the beginning. If Evans' teachings suggest that Simples should marry each other for the sake of purity, maybe that's why my marriage failed. No matter how hard I tried, I could never devote my whole heart to Richard. Without question, I can do that for Abraham. I want to be bound to him. I want to obey him.

21

"They live healthy, productive lives, because of Evans' mercy."

    Word about The Discomfort is spreading quickly. In between cooking and cleaning, all I can think about is checking my phone. There are dozens of messages, and even more comments. Every notification alerts all of my senses. The number of followers is growing steadily, too. People are curious about me, and it's hard not to feel flattered. Yes, the group is getting greater visibility, but most people are talking about me.
    Sure, there is outrage. Some call me vile names, and say all kinds of horrible things should happen to me. I just block and report them. I love the ease of that. In real life, I have to put up with the things and people that bother me. I have to be submissive. Online, I can be dismissive and dominant. I can look at other people's photos and comments as often as I want. So many people post about every thought in their head, and let strangers into their daily whereabouts. I know where they live, who is in their families,

what their interests are, and how they see themselves. It feels like ownership. I have pieces of them that they'll never have of me.

Those who don't reach out to threaten me, on the other hand, are full of encouragement. They tell me how amazing and courageous I am. They've been waiting their whole lives for someone like me. My safety matters to them. I inspire them. Some even say I look pretty.

I never saw myself as pretty, and I'm not used to being complimented. I learned that praise in one's appearance and completion of tasks ends in selfishness. I know I should think more about the movement and finding those girls. At the same time, the personal attention feels so good. I want more of it. Since the live video did so well, I plan on recording another one.

***

I'm in bed. My door is open- as always, but I know Jaxtyn and Quinn are asleep. They're heavy sleepers that snore. I'll still keep my voice down, or maybe I should try the closet. Yeah. I think I'll do that instead. I get up with my phone, grab a flashlight, and go into the closet. I sit down. It's cramped, but I have an extra sound barrier to protect me. I keep the flashlight on, clear my throat, log into my account, and prepare another live video.

"Hello, everyone. This is Gertrude, again, on behalf of The Discomfort. I have some important information about Comfort for Community. A brave woman has come forward with her story. She doesn't want to say her name, so I'm going to respect that. She did give me permission to share her story, though.

"She was pregnant, and in an abusive relationship. The only way she could get out was to run away and hide. She believed that Comfort for Community would provide some kind of protection for her and her baby. Instead, she was told that she didn't belong. Her name was changed, her color code was changed, and she was forced to take abortion pills. Her husband was arrested, but not for abuse. His crime was having anything to do with her. The woman was then put on a plane, and forced into another family. The new family was given a fake origin story, and the government told her she'd always be under surveillance. That's why she can't be in the video.

"Comfort for Community did not protect her. The program lures Blended people into police stations to kidnap them, reclassify them, force abortions, and fly them off to new families. Their pasts are erased, and they become property of the government. President Evans is 100% behind the trafficking of Blended people. The program needs to be stopped."

As soon as I finish recording, my serious expression becomes a grin. My video is going to get a lot of attention. At first, I didn't like the idea of Comfort for Community ending. Now, I see it's best that it does. As long as the government keeps tabs on me, I'm stuck with the Clarks. I'd have to marry David, and be everything he wants me to be. If I run away, I risk arrest... or worse.

***

I wake up.

It's the same old routine. Jaxtyn gets his big, wasted breakfast, then I mentally prepare for some more housework. Only, as soon as the man leaves the driveway, Quinn has something to tell me. She sits me down on the couch.

"We have a problem."

"What's going on, Mom?"

"That terrorist group started a social media page. David messaged Jaxtyn about it this morning. There's a girl on there... a Blended... spreading all kinds of propaganda against Simples."

"Really? What is she saying?"

"She's making it sound like Nicole was kidnapped... as if Simples are savages. She also has her facts wrong about that black David grabbed. For some reason, she's blaming a Two. Not sure where she's getting her information. She's also saying scandalous things about the Comfort law. It's not a federal law, but she's blaming Evans. She's a whole mess. People like her want to see the whole country fall apart. She needs to be arrested for treason, as well as her illegal birth."

"What... what can we do?"

"Our dear Evans has already responded. That girl makes it sound as if Blended people are in danger. Far from it. They shouldn't be here, but those who *are* are grateful. They live healthy, productive lives, because of Evans' mercy. Proof is in our very own Constitution. He fought for our right to vote however we want. Repealed the 22nd Amendment by ratifying the 28th Amendment... allowing the American people to vote for candidates as much as we want to. He did that, and the people have spoken. That's why he's serving his 5th term in a row."

I remember Evan's 5th presidential inauguration well, because I was married off that same year.

Quinn continues, "Many of the Blended are our allies. Evans is encouraging them to tell their stories online, using #simplicityworks. So far, the response has been big. Hopefully, big enough to drown out that awful girl, and her destructive lies."

"Yes, Mom. Hopefully."

I couldn't wait to check my phone. Throughout the day, I peeked at it. I had so many notifications. Unfortunately, it wasn't until bedtime I was able to really read everything.

Comments under my second video are even more heated. Either they're insulting me, or sharing their personal stories having to do with Comfort for Community. Cops, nurses, doctors, family members, witnesses… all kinds of people. I knew the reactions would be strong, but I'm surprised by the decrease of personal attention I'm getting. No one is complimenting me. No one is cheering me on.

Maybe it's because no one can see my face that well. I won't make any more videos in the dark. In fact, it's now I realize I didn't have my makeup or wig on, so I'm glad I was in the dark. I can't believe that slipped my mind. I really need to be careful. But yes, makeup and good daytime lighting will allow people to see me better.

I decide to search for that hashtag, #simplicityworks. Quinn was right. The response is huge. Blended people from all over the country are talking about how great their lives are, and how thankful they are to live in the United States. Some of them are saying The Discomfort is a terrorist group, and Comfort for Community is saving lives. Looking at the comments, many are accusing the hashtag users of being Twos. I wonder how that's going to work for them. Twos seem to operate best when no one can pick them out of a crowd. Maybe the hashtag was supposed to ruin The Discomfort's credibility, but Evans has effectively encouraged so many Twos to blow their cover.

Suddenly, I get a text notification from Abraham. It reads:

Effing brilliant. Simples showing true colors. U speak out, Evans throws all Blended under bus. 2s have nowhere to go.

I laugh, and send a text back:

All that ass kissing to be thrown to the wolves. We should adopt them.

He texts:

Ur amazing, G

I reread the text over and over in my head, fully aware of the goofy grin on my face. Finally and without a doubt, Abraham is truly mine. I lay down in bed, envisioning him beside me. I imagine the warmth of his skin radiating on me, and the firm touch of his hand. I love how the bass of his voice makes my whole body vibrate. I want his brown skin to caress my bare white skin until it darkens. I want his fingers to darken and curl my straight blonde hair. I want him to call me Gertrude, because he knows that's my real name. I want to cross the Gate, and never look back.

I'm inspired to post something new. I text Abraham:

Simps shouldn't have access 2 us. Need 2 block gate.
How?
Our bodies. Word of mouth or DM. No public posts. Next Friday.
Why Friday?
Work, travel. Will wanna pass gate. They wanna be separate anyway. Text/msg everyone.
On it.

I'm going to keep Quinn and Jaxtyn in the dark this time. I want to catch them, and the Simple Watch completely off guard. I want to observe them in the way I do people online. I love the feeling of putting something out there for others to feed off of. I wield the unique power of exposing weaknesses within the Simples, and making the Blended want to follow my lead. Next week, everyone will witness that power. I hope it's felt far beyond the Lowlands. With enough attention, I might be able to intimidate the president into ending Comfort for Community.

22

"Well, things are getting a little too dangerous."

It's showtime. I drive to the Lowlands pool parking lot. I get out and wait next to my car. Before breakfast, I made up an emergency Simple Watch meeting that I needed to go to. Quinn and Jaxtyn amazingly let me go- without question. I feel as if I'm the one who runs the house now. Jaxtyn is no threat.

All he does is work, waste food, and not clean up after himself. He's oblivious about the world beyond what he has a direct hand in, and his own wife is able to keep secrets from him. He's useless in the way my husband was. He only earned his position through birthright. He pays the bills, but there are no bills without a home. No place to put groceries, no reason for lights, and no running water. A man needs a home, and he needs a woman to maintain it. He needs that woman to feed him, spread his seed, then he needs to make that woman fearful of him. After today, I will be the one who is feared.

Lindsay and Jonathan pull up in their sedan, right next to me. As soon as Lindsay gets out of the car, she rushes over to hug me.

"I can't believe this is happening. Are you nervous?"

"A little." I'm lying. I assume it's what she needs to hear me say.

She takes a deep breath. "Me, too."

"I'm surprised Abraham isn't here yet," says Jonathan. "He left before us."

That's interesting information. "Before you?"

Lindsay nods in agreement. "The only reason we know is because he moved in with us. He didn't want any of our activities to put his parents in danger. I guess they're reconciling, too. Anyways, he left before we did. Didn't say anything about running errands or anything. Figured he drove straight here."

"Hmm. That is weird."

I wonder why he didn't tell me about his parents, or moving in with the other Discomfort members. I didn't realize they were that close. What else is he hiding from me? What else do Lindsay and Jonathan know that I don't? Where is he, what is he up to, and who is he with!?

Just then, another sedan pulls up next to Lindsay and Jonathan's car. It's Abraham. Part of me is happy to see him, but another part of me feels guarded and irritated. He gets out of his car. Jonathan greets him, then Lindsay. He looks at me with a sweet smile. I instinctively smile back. I can't help it. He walks over to give me a big hug, and a sweet kiss.

Jonathan smirks. "So… This is kind of a double date."

We collectively groan and laugh. With Lindsay holding her boyfriend's hand, and me holding mine, we walk towards the Gate. This is when I first start to look around me. More and more people are trickling in, and we can see some are already at the Gate. Some have signs. Many are taking pictures. I see families, interracial couples, and even Simples.

A small group of Simple girls catches my eye especially. With their covered bodies, updos, and lack of accessories, they're easy to point out. What brought them here? Who told them about today? How did they learn about each other? They look around my age, so I assume they're married. Maybe they even have a child or two. I'm sure their husbands think they're tending to the home right now. I had to lie, and hide my skin and hair to come here. They arrived as is. Why is everyone okay with their presence? I feel like I'm the only person who is fascinated by them.

Lindsay squeals. "This is way more diverse than I thought it would be. I had no idea so many people cared."

I physically match her reaction, but I can't shake a growing annoyance. I'm not sure why I feel this way. Abraham has his arm around my waist, while my mind is gathering memories of feeling alone and like a burden. He's grinning from ear to ear. I'm supposed to be just as elated right now. What's wrong with me?

I instinctively pull out my phone, and go straight to my app.

"Plan on taking pictures?" asks Jonathan.

"No. I think I want to make a live video."

Abraham's expression changes. "If you post live, people will know what's going on as it happens. They'll be able to recognize the location, and plan an attack."

"It made sense to be quiet *before*, yeah. But *during*… We need the world to see this. Besides, look around you. People are already taking pictures and recording videos. If anyone was planning on coming over here to start trouble, it's already out of our hands. Look at the impact we've created. We should show ourselves… be unafraid."

"But…," Lindsay interjects. "Faces will be recognized. If not today, retaliation can come later. I'm not comfortable being on camera."

"Leave me out of it, too," says Jonathan. "Pictures with blurred out faces, and after the fact… I get. A live video has too many risks."

I shrug. "Okay. I'll be in the shot, then. Like always. People need to see this... from us."

I move away from the group, so they're nowhere near my shot. I have the Gate behind me, and the camera phone lens in front of me. There's something about that lens that's so comforting. It can't furrow its brow at me, or change the tone of its voice. It can't hit me, or discard me. It focuses on me, and lets me speak. I hit record.

"Good morning, everyone! This is Gertrude from The Discomfort. We have something special happening right now. A bunch of us are gathered at our Gate today. Simples are up the hill. Many are about to head to work. In order to do that, they need to cross the Gate, and drive through our neighborhood to go downtown. This area used to be fully integrated, until Evans took over, and Simples took to the hill. They can pass through our space, but we can never enter theirs. Today, they will have no choice but to deal with us."

I sense people around me gathering, and watching through their own camera lenses. I use my phone to scan the crowd. Those who don't turn away, wave and cheer.

"Let's block this Gate, guys!"

The crowd cheers as we all congest the road that goes through the wooded area. We can see cars coming. I continue filming as the roar of the crowd gets louder, and the cars come to a complete stop. I focus the camera back on my face.

"If you're here with us... in spirit or in person, make sure to post your pictures and videos. Tag us, because we want to see you, and use #abrilandbarbara. That's a-b-r-i-l-a-n-d-b-a-r-b-a-r-a.

All one word, no caps. Abril should be here. Barbara should be here. *We* should be here. This Gate should not."

Abraham gives me a thumbs up. I'm so overcome by the energy of the crowd, the encouraging comments on my feed, and Abraham's admiration, I run to him while the camera is still filming. Keeping the camera pointed at myself, I give him a kiss. He instantly flinches away. I realize that I accidentally showed part of his face. I'll make it right by proving how harmless that was. He's being really silly about the whole thing.

"Guys, that was my boyfriend- another member of The Discomfort. We're out here making history… as a Blended couple out in the open."

Abraham shakes his head at me. I just shrug and laugh. I tried making the best of a mild lapse in judgment. It's not like I plan on telling people his name. I hope that moment was noticed by enough people, though. They'll recognize him, and know he belongs to me. I stop recording, upload the video, then put my phone away.

All of us are standing in place, watching traffic build up on the 2-lane road. The men are honking their horns, waving their fists, and yelling all kinds of obscenities. Something compels me to move forward. The other members of The Discomfort don't want to show their faces on camera- much less to the Simples in their cars. I move my way through the crowd, placing myself in the direct line of vision of the driver in front.

I've never looked this intensely into a man's eyes before. In the past, such an action would've gotten me smacked. This guy can easily run me over with his car, but he's choosing not to. I am valuable in this situation. While focused on him, I'm well aware that many others are focused on me. That includes the group of

Simple girls. My adrenaline is pumping. I have nothing planned. I can't think of a speech, a clever thing to say, or a harmful insult. I'm just standing in place. For everyone, that seems to be enough. Again, camera phones are aimed at me. The crowd hushes in anticipation. I need to give them something. Anything.

With my eyes still glued to the driver, I slowly raise up one arm, and point up the hill. I hold the position for as long as I can, so it looks less obvious that I have no idea what I'm doing. In the corner of my eye, I see other protestors make the same gesture. Gradually, they all do.

I have no idea how much time is passing. I want to say 10 minutes, but maybe it just feels that long. The drivers are still yelling and honking, but it all sounds muffled. Suddenly, the driver decides to make a 3-point turn back up the hill. Begrudgingly, the drivers behind him do the same. I have no idea how that worked.

The crowd cheers. My mind is still processing what just happened, as people high 5 and hug me. They ask to take pictures with me, and want to follow me online. One woman even cries in my arms. I have no idea where the other members are, and I'm not too eager to find them. I figure they don't want to be seen anyway. I'm doing them a favor by keeping all the attention on myself.

Eventually, I get to look at my phone. The hashtag I made up is already trending, and The Discomfort has been tagged many times. My videos are being screenshot and reposted. I'm everywhere. Everyone is dying to know about the Blended girl in North California named Gertrude.

***

I wait until the crowd dies down, but that doesn't happen until the afternoon. Going to the Gate to wipe off my makeup, and take off my wig isn't an option today, either. I have to find a quiet street in the Lowlands to park, and do what I need to. Then, I can drive back up the hill with no issues.

I expect the front door to open as soon as I pull up to the driveway. That's not happening. I unlock the door. No one is behind it. The whole house is quiet.

"Sir? Ma'am?"

No response. I walk to the living room. I see Quinn and Jaxtyn sitting on the couch and watching the news. They're seeing footage of today's protest. A banner on the TV screen reads:

Comfort for Community no longer providing refuge to Blended.

"Wait. What?"

I'm realizing I said that out loud, and it startles the couple. They had no idea I had just come home.

Jaxtyn grumbles. "Is that what your emergency meeting was about?"

"Yes, Sir. We tried to mobilize quickly and stop it. We couldn't. What's that about Comfort for Community? If I may ask, Sir?"

"Evans gave an inspiring speech today. He reminded people that the Blended are illegal. They're lucky they get to live in this country, and the special care they receive is unfair to us real Americans. For a group that claims to want equality so bad, they have a hard time looking out for other people. A bunch of us missed out on some pay today."

"I'm not sure I understand, Sir."

"They introduced a bill making it a federal crime to deny jail time for the Blended on any grounds. No more leniency programs. Everyone is confident that it will pass, and Evans will sign it. Comfort laws won't be able to exist anymore."

"I saw Simples in that riot footage," bursts Quinn. "Young women... probably unmarried and bitter."

"They better be from out of town, if they know what's good for them," Jaxtyn adds.

Quinn gets up, and walks over to me. She moves her arms out for a hug, then stops herself. "What information do you have for us?"

"It's sensitive, Ma'am. We're up to something, though."

"Well, things are getting a little too dangerous. David's birthday is in a handful of days. Once we marry you off, you can step away from all of this. You've been a wonderful caretaker to the community, but women belong at home. Let your husband provide, and be a soldier for the cause."

"Does this mean I need to stop going to meetings, Ma'am?"

Jaxtyn responds. "One more meeting. You can go say your goodbyes, then that's it. You're going to be a wife soon, and a mother."

"Yes, Sir."

"By the way, another package from the agency came for you. It's in your room."

"Thank you, Sir. Excuse me, Sir and Ma'am."

I walk over to my bedroom to see the large cardboard box on the floor. It's a very welcomed sight. I immediately tear off the tape, open the flaps, and gaze at a new supply of hair dye and Enlightenment. Next on my list is to reach out to Amanda for the final time.

23

"Can I still follow you online?"

David's birthday is in just a few days.

Today, I'm going to my last fake Simple Watch Meeting. Jaxtyn has already left for work. Quinn is cleaning the kitchen. I have my usual stuff ready, but I want to bring one more thing along. I sneak into the Clarks' bedroom, then their walk-in closet. I'm pretty sure of what I'll find there.

On Jaxtyn's side is an accessible arsenal of a few guns and hunting knives. I grab the largest serrated knife he has. "J. Clark" is engraved on the handle. That couldn't be more perfect. I stuff it in my purse, carefully walk out of their bedroom, then rush down the stairs. The stomping noise I make catches Quinn's attention. She walks towards me at the front door.

"Have a good meeting, honey. If things run late, just come home. Your duty there is done anyway."

"Okay, Mom."

With that, she sends me off with a warm, lingering hug. I wonder how she took care of her need for affection before I arrived. Was she ever able to? I'm already losing focus.

"Love you, honey."

"Love you too, Mom." Just words. I can only ever let them be words.

I walk out the front door. In what feels like slow motion, I get into the car, then start the ignition. I take the time to really observe the neighborhood as I drive through. This is the last time I will see it in the daylight. Part of me will almost miss it, but I have no idea why.

I drive to the Gate and park in the lot. As always, no one is around. I scan the area as I put my makeup and wig on, but not just to see if anyone is watching. I want to get a mental picture of the area during daylight hours.

I never noticed how vividly green the tree leaves are, or how beautiful the wildflowers are. I hear birds conversing, and the rustling of the leaves in the breeze. There are no voices, and no hint of buildings. It feels as if I'm the only human on earth. I'm not, though. I regain focus on the task at hand. I place my knife, wallet and makeup with the gun in the glove compartment. Now, off to the pool.

***

As soon as I park my car, I realize the mistake I was about to make. I'm too familiar now. I can't go to the restroom without my plan failing. Thankfully, Amanda is already nearby. She recognizes me, and walks to the car. She presents me with an awkward smile. I know she feels obligated. I can't expect her to be excited to see me. We're both getting something out of this, though. I need the money, and she wants to get herself out of a jam. It will all be over soon.

The teen opens the door, and gets into the passenger seat. "Morning, Dinah."

"Morning, Amanda. How are you?"

"Good. I've been seeing you online and stuff. I knew about the block-in, but I was too nervous to go. Looks like there was a huge turnout. Even the president knows about The Discomfort now."

I laugh. "Yeah, it's pretty cool."

"Good idea calling yourself by a different name, too."

"Thanks. So... I have good news and bad news."

"Okay."

I put on my best encouraging face. "My source had a change of heart. They're going to let both of us go."

"Really!?"

"Yes, but... You have to sell one last time."

Amanda visibly deflates. "You... You mean one tub?"

I shake my head. "One day. They are giving you till the end of today to sell 12 tubs."

She hesitates. I can tell her mind is spinning, and she- more than likely- wants to cry. I can't let her break down on me. I speak sternly to snap her out of whatever she has going on.

"You don't trust me?"

"I... I trust you."

"Did I come back for you like I said I would?"

"Yes."

"Am I helping you out of this?"

"Yes?"

"*Yes*, I am. At the end of the day, they call the shots, but they *are* letting you go. They put this obligation on you, because they know you can do it. I know you can, too. I think very highly of you, Amanda. Your hard work is not only going to earn you and I money. You're going to set us free. If you don't do this, we're both bound to them for as long as they say. So don't you start crying for yourself. I'm just as stuck in this as you are."

The teen takes in a deep breath through her nose, then exhales out her mouth. "Okay."

"Good. I'm going to leave you with this." I hand her my bag. "You have until 6 P.M. to sell all 12 tubs. Depending on how much you make, you might be able to take a couple grand home. Understand?"

She nods.

I smile, then give her a warm, lingering hug- much like the one I received this morning. I'm not sure why.

"You can do this."

Amanda nods again, then gets out of the car. She drags herself to the restroom. She's far less eager than last time, but she's also far more desperate. I know she'll perform just fine.

***

I drive over to Jonathan and Lindsay's apartment. I'm especially excited to see Abraham. We haven't seen each other since the protest, but we've been messaging each other a lot. He finally opened up about his family life. His problems are so foreign to me. It's hard to distinguish what is normal, and when I should console him.

At first, my mind fought tuning him out to save itself from overthinking. I soon learned to just say very little, and give the illusion of being a good listener. It worked, because he had a lot to say. I learned that he spends a lot of quality time with his parents. He checks in with them every morning and night. They're informal, and almost sound equal to one another. The only big issue is none of them can be seen together. That was causing a lot of stress in the marriage and household, but they're working it out. Must be nice.

I've never been to an apartment. The idea of strangers living on top of each other in an enclosed space sounds like some kind of infection. There's no land- just walls. They basically live on a deserted island. I guess I kind of know what that feels like.

I knock on their door. Lindsay answers.

"Dinah! I'm so happy to see you." She escorts me in. "Are you thirsty? Would you like anything to snack on?"

"I'm fine. Thank you."

The guys are sitting on the couch together. When they see me walk in, they stand up. Abraham walks over to give me a kiss. Somehow, it doesn't feel as magical as it used to. I smile brightly at him anyway. It would look weird if I didn't.

The four of us move to the dining room table. It's just big enough to fit all of us. Abraham and I sit across from Lindsay and Jonathan.

I start off with the good news. "We did it, you guys."

"Did what?" asks Abraham.

"Huh? I know you've been watching the news. The Comfort law is officially done."

Lindsay sighs. "Without the Comfort law in place, Abril will be in limbo. It will be a lot harder to find her."

I hold in my groan, and prevent my eyes from rolling. They're getting what they wanted. Why is she being so negative?

I shrug. "I mean… we know a Simple named David is responsible. Let's start there."

"How many Simples named David are out there?" asks Jonathan. "That information tells us nothing."

"But Evans ending Comfort for Community isn't nothing. We exposed the truth. We called him out, and he totally caved in."

Abraham raises an eyebrow. "So quickly, though?"

"I mean- "

Jonathan cuts me off. "He denied having anything to do with it for years. Now, he's taking credit for ending it. The law was bullshit, but- at least- it pretended to benefit us. Now, there's no more pretending."

"He's up to something." Lindsay says under her breath.

I shake my head. "Evans isn't a calculating person. He's hardcore about Simplicity. Nothing is dragged out, and nothing is looming."

Jonathan shakes his head back. "Simple, to Evans, means it makes sense to him- not that it lacks any complication or planning."

"Gert, I mean…." I look at Abraham- who I know is not about to defend me. "He said- more than once- he had nothing to do with the law. He did. The whole time. That's pretty calculating."

Jonathan nods. "On everyone's part. The governor who spearheaded the law back then *allegedly* wasn't a Simple."

I'm dumbfounded. They got what they wanted, and the battle wasn't as hard as they thought. Do they prefer a challenge? Are they upset, because they feel less oppressed? Do they not know what to do with themselves now? Out of all of us, I'm the one who directly experienced the effects of the law. I came out fine. If there was a refuge program for Simples or abused women in general, I would have opted for that. No one cares about us, though. Without any fuss, a bunch of governors started a program that enabled Blended people to avoid jail time. They were given a chance, but it was suspicious. Now that the law is ending, *that's* suspicious.

Abraham holds my hand. I think he can feel my energy.

He says, "Look… I don't want to be all doom and gloom, either. But… we have been given multiple reasons to tread carefully. We need to keep our eyes all the way open."

I nod reassuringly. In truth, I'm so annoyed, I can hardly hear him. This is going to be a long meeting.

***

The sun is beginning to set. I leave the apartment, and drive back to the pool. Amanda is waiting for me at the parking lot. She looks nervous. I really hope she sold everything, because I really need the money. If she failed, I'm going to be stuck making a tough decision. I can't look like a liar.

Amanda gets in the passenger seat.

I try my best to seem calm. "So, how did it go?"

She hands me my purse. It's empty. She sold everything!

"That stuff was never more popular than it was today."

"Really!? What did you earn?"

"$3600."

"That's fantastic, Amanda!"

She hands me the money. "Does this really mean I'm done?"

"Yes. You never have to sell again, and this will be our last time meeting up."

Amanda looks shocked. I'm not sure why. After everything, I figured she'd be relieved not to see me anymore. What's with Blended people, and the prospect of being left alone? I pull out some cash- $1000, to be completely exact. I put the money in her hand.

"That's two grand for your troubles."

The sight of the money isn't cheering her up. I add, "You're free now."

Amanda just looks at me, as if she's waiting for something, but I'm not sure what. She's hardly looking at the money, so I know it's not about me shorting her. I brighten my facial expression, but hers doesn't change.

"You're free, Amanda."

Slowly, her face does change, but now she's crying. All I can do is stare back at her. My body is totally rigid. I have no idea what to say or do, and that angers me. As far as she knows, I helped her out of a serious situation. I saved her life. I could have

166

used her for a lot longer. I need more money, but this will have to do.

I pull out every ounce of sweetness and patience that I have left. "I'll always remember you. It's been a crazy ride, but now I'm needed elsewhere. And I know you'll be okay."

Amanda sniffles, reaching for the glove compartment. I grab her hand before she's able to open it.

"What are you doing?"

"I just… Do you have any tissues?"

"I don't."

She sucks in her snot, and wipes what's left. "Can I still follow you online?"

I shrug my shoulders. "Sure. In a way, it isn't goodbye then."

"Okay."

"Bye."

"... Bye."

The teen takes her time stepping out of the car. She still looks as if she wants to tell me something, but I'm not going to force it out of her. I wouldn't know what to do with the information if I had it. When she finally gets out and closes the door, I drive off.

I'm on the lookout for a quiet area. Eventually, I find an empty parking lot. I use the space to wash off my makeup, and take off my wig. I stuff Jaxtyn's hunting knife in my oversized dress pocket. I put my phone in the opposite pocket. My next stop is at the Gate. I'm ready to meet my future husband.

24

"You can be mine in this moment."

The sun is completely out of sight now. I park in the abandoned lot at the Gate, then honk the horn. A handful of flashlights gradually emerge through the trees, and gather around me. Taking a deep breath, I step out of the vehicle. The lights hover over my body and blind me.

"David? Is there a David here?"

I hear murmurs. The lights move to reveal several shadowy figures, but one sticks out. It's nearest to me, but not close enough for me to see exactly who it is.

The shadow addresses me with a deep male voice. "What business do you have out here? You should be home."

"David is my business, Sir. My name is Dinah. I belong to Jaxtyn Clark, Sir."

The shadow moves even closer toward me before flashing the light on his face. He's a middle-aged brunette with thick facial hair and a grin.

"Oh, yeah. He told me all about you."

"Yes, Sir. He wants to present me as a gift for your birthday, Sir."

"Hmm. I assume he doesn't know you're here?"

"You are correct, Sir."

David looks to the other figures in the dark. "Carry on, guys. I'll deal with her."

Without a word, the lights move back into the thickness of the trees. It's just him and me now.

He grabs my wrist. "Is this how you are? You think it's okay to sneak off without a man's approval?"

"Well, Sir… My father won't have control of me much longer. I'm practically yours already. I've been very eager to meet you, and receive your guidance, Sir. I'm sorry for my disobedience. I'll go straight home and admit what I've done, Sir."

He still has a firm hold of me. "Don't worry about it. I'll set things straight with him. He already gave his blessing. You can be mine in this moment."

"I can, Sir?"

"Follow me."

"Yes, Sir."

By the wrist, he pulls me into the woods. His pace suggests that he knows exactly where he's going. I've never explored this area, and the darkness is disorienting. My heart is racing. I look to the stars as some kind of proof that I'm not alone. I can feel my eyes want to well up, but I don't let them. I don't want David to see, and be upset by my reaction.

All of a sudden, David pushes me up against a tree. He throws his lips against mine with such great force, it feels hateful. Richard seemed loving at first. Over time, he became mean. David isn't one to waste time. As he pulls my hair back, and roughly kisses my neck, I scramble for the hunting knife in my pocket. I get a hold of the handle. With as much strength as I can gather, I shove the knife into his neck as I pull away.

I gasp as he drops his flashlight. I can see the knife almost completely in the shadow's neck. He's feeling around the handle and gurgling. Without a second thought, I pull the knife out, and begin stabbing him wildly. I can't tell exactly where the knife is going or how deep. His body falls to the ground, but I continue to stab him. I don't even know why I'm carrying on, and all I can hear is my rapid breathing.

At some point, I realize the shadow isn't moving, and the gurgling has stopped. I'm not sure for how long that has been the case. I stand up, leaving the knife inside him.

"Leave me alone."

I take his flashlight, and then reach for my phone. I log in, and hit the record button. One hand is pointing the flashlight on David's body, while the other hand is pointing the lens at him. Off camera, I speak with a soft voice- so I'm not easily heard by the other shadows at the Gate.

"This is Gertrude with The Discomfort. An unnamed source has led me to this location. Out of fear of retaliation, I can not reveal that source. I also can't reveal the location. This is the body of David, the Simple responsible for kidnapping Abril, and forcing her into the Comfort for Community program. His killer left the weapon behind. The engraving reads 'J. Clark'. It is believed to be another Simple. I repeat: Abril's kidnapper was killed by another Simple."

I calmly find my way back to the lot. Turns out we didn't walk very far. It sure felt like it at the time. As I approach my car, no other flashlights are around. I get in, and drive up the hill. I know blood is splattered all over me. That's fine. That won't matter when all is said and done.

***

I pull into the Clarks' driveway. Immediately, Quinn runs out. I step out of the vehicle. I'm not even stressed, but she sure is.

"Where have you been? What happened to you!?"

Jaxtyn is standing at the doorway. "Both of you... inside... NOW."

Quinn rushes inside, while I take my time. I don't care anymore. When I move into the light of the indoors, I hear gasps at the sight of me.

"What happened!?" Jaxtyn looks more furious than concerned.

"Was the Watch meeting attacked?" Quinn leans in, almost as if she wants to hold me.

I shake my head. "David... He's dead."

The couple is speechless. I want to smile, but I force a horrified expression as I turn towards Quinn.

"I had to see for myself. I didn't think you'd actually do it."

She's taken aback. "What are you going on about, Dinah?"

"You told me how badly you wanted a girl, and how good it feels to have power over someone. A daughter can never surpass you, but I *can* leave you."

I then turn to Jaxtyn. "She's so unhappy. Complains about you all the time. Said she'd harm all of my suitors, if I ever considered them. I'd be of no use to the Greater Good. I wanted to handle the matter privately, so as not to upset you. That's why I joined the Simple Watch. I needed to surround myself with dutiful women, so I can be a proper Simple. I didn't want her to poison me."

"You lying bitch!" Quinn slaps me across the face.

I look right into her eyes, as I continue to address her husband. "Do you know why she's so unhappy?"

"Speak."

I redirect my gaze towards Jaxtyn, his face red at this point. I reach into my purse, and hand Quinn's still-loaded gun to him.

"What are you doing with this?" he asks.

"I bet she made you think she couldn't have a child. Well, she can. Ask about her *first* husband, and the baby she carried for him."

Quinn grabs my arm in a panic. "Why are you doing this? Please stop. Please! Please tell him you're lying!"

I give her a look of disgust. "For the sake of the Greater Good, I will no longer protect you."

Quinn lets go of my arm, ready to cry. I calmly turn around, and walk back outside. I leave the door wide open. On the way to the car, I can hear Quinn sobbing and pleading. Then, I hear screaming. I get back into the car, and pull out of the driveway. There is a gunshot, then complete silence.

I feel regret, but it dissipates as quickly as it's felt. Quinn meant me harm- just like the rest of them. Like my biological mother, she was willing to marry me off to a maniac. I was going to end up right back where I started. I couldn't allow that. I'm not a bad person. I did what I had to survive. Quinn was guilty of that, too.

I keep driving until I get to the Gate. Subconsciously, I park at the lot. Everything feels still. I assume the other Simple Watch members within the trees haven't discovered David's body yet. I wish I could set all of this on fire, but I have nothing on me. Instead, I pull out my phone. There are dozens of notifications, but I read none of them. Instead, I take a random picture of the dark sky, and leave a post. The caption reads:

David's body is at the Gate

I pull out a water bottle. I use the light from my cell phone to help me rinse the blood from my visible skin. I can't do anything about the blood on my clothes right now. I apply makeup as carefully as I can, and tuck my hair beneath my curly wig. Then, I calmly put my phone back into my purse.

I take a good look at myself in the rearview mirror, despite the heavy darkness. The ends of my lips begin to curl. I'm now laughing hysterically. At first, it feels like a release. Moments later, I feel uneasy. I'm not sure what I'm even laughing at, and I'm worried about calling attention to myself. Still, it's difficult to calm down. I do manage to wrangle my laughter in, but it leaves my body with little energy to do anything else.

I stare ahead for a few long minutes, not focusing on anything in particular. I then close my eyes. It's so quiet. With each gentle exhale, I release tension throughout my muscles. I soon find myself resting my head against the car window. A few tears fall, but I don't feel sad. I feel numb. Slowly, I pull myself back up. Right on time, I start the ignition as the glare of flashlights returns.

Everyone and everything that has ever held me back is gone. What happens now is completely up to me. All I want to do now is return to my home in the Lowlands.

25

"If you can't trust us, then we're already losing."

    I know I'm arriving unannounced, but I don't see them turning me away. In actuality, I see them celebrating me. I found Abril's kidnapper. I exposed him to the world, and made him pay for what he did.
    I knock on the apartment door. Abraham answers, and gives me a look that's less than enthusiastic.
    "You don't answer your phone anymore? At least, I know what the blood on your clothes is about."
    "Huh?"
    I take a look at my phone. Turns out he tried calling me 5 times, and left just as many text messages. I shrug my shoulders as I walk in. I'm here now, anyway. Lindsay and Jonathan are sitting on the couch.
    "I'm so sorry. My phone was on silent. Everyone's still awake?"
    Abraham scoffs. "You've been on your phone, though."
    Jonathan looks really annoyed, too. "What happened!? Why did you post that shit?"

"People have a right to know. We were looking for the guy anyway."

Lindsay is the calmest of the bunch. "Who told you where he was?"

"I... I'm really sorry, but I can't say."

Abraham shakes his head. "General public, we understand. You should be able to tell *us*. Did the source know David's whereabouts while he was still alive?"

I laugh. "Who cares at this point? He's dead, and a Simple is responsible. Everyone up the hill knew about him. I wouldn't be surprised if he was murdered by one of the Simple allies at the block-in."

"That doesn't make sense," says Lindsay. "Without him, we can't find Abril. He's no good to us dead. Besides, we want justice- not revenge. Whoever killed him isn't associated with us."

Jonathan adds, "And what was the point of filming his body, and telling people where the body is? We look like instigators. You could have reported the facts without a morbid video, and telling the whole world where to take a photo op. That kind of stunt ruins our credibility."

I throw my bag to the ground. "Why are you all mad at me!? I did what I thought was right at the time. The media goes out of its way to keep people in the dark. People have a right to know who April's kidnapper was, and what happened to him."

Lindsay sighs. "People want to know what happened to *Abril*, Dinah."

"I stand behind what I did. Have you even looked at the responses? Here." I take out my phone, and hand it to Abraham. "Look for yourself."

Abraham clicks on the app. I'm already signed in. I have no idea what he's going to see, because I haven't had a chance to look myself. I'm desperate, though. The Discomfort is all I have left, and they're already turning on me. I guess I'm not as free as I thought I was. I still need others to find value in me. I thought being a Blended gave me more value than being a Simple, but now it feels no different. I'm out of place, unwelcome and inconvenient.

Abraham looks at the phone for what feels like forever. He finally says, "First of all, I've never seen so many notifications. Over 40 new followers, 20 messages, almost 80 likes, a couple dozen comments, and a whole lot of tags."

Jonathan moves in to get a closer look. "What are they tagging us on?"

Abraham shuffles through the posts. "People are talking about that Clark guy. He's been arrested. Simple Watch already knew about him, and where to find him. He killed his wife, too."

Lindsay gasps. "That's crazy. I wonder why he did all that."

"Doesn't matter why," says Abraham. "You know Evans is going to make an example out of him. They can't hide him and pretend no crime was committed. Too many people are watching."

I cross my arms. "Well... It sure is a good thing I made such a big deal about it."

"Dinah, we're just worried," says Lindsay. "A lot has happened in a short period of time. The cafe was burned down. I'm lucky to have something else lined up, but we can't all get by with one salary. We still don't know where Barbara is. Abril will be even harder to find now. Yeah, our block-in was successful, but its impact will drown in the news of two Simples getting murdered. We're on Evan's radar now, too. It's important to be careful how we come across... for our safety, and the clarity of our mission."

Jonathan nods. "Next time someone comes to you with some kind of information, share it with all of us before posting anything. And tell us who the source is. There should be no secrets between us."

"But, Jonathan, I promised to protect the person's identity. I can't go back on my word."

"You're not the only member of The Discomfort. If you can't trust us, then we're already losing."

I look down. "Speaking of trust… I can't exactly go home now. I need a place to stay. That's why I'm here."

"You're welcome to stay," Lindsay says after some hesitation. "Right, Jonathan?"

Jonathan nods. He's smiling at me, but there's a bit of uncertainty in his eyes. "Yes. You are welcome here, and you're safe here."

Lindsay continues. "We only have one bedroom, so Abraham sleeps on a cot in the living room. I don't think either of you will mind sharing. Bring your things in, and we can get you settled."

"I just have my purse."

There's more hesitation. The three of them look at each other with concern.

Abraham is the one to speak up. "You must have left in a hurry. Everything okay?"

"Anything else you need to let us in on?" adds Jonathan.

I sigh. "Like you said… a lot has happened in a short period of time. I have the added benefit of a recognizable face. I just need a place to stay. Not for very long, and I promise to not be any trouble."

Lindsay half smiles. "Ok. Well… please get comfortable. You can use my soap, and any towel. I have a few extra bonnets, too. They're in a drawer in the bathroom. Help yourself. I think I'm going to call it a night."

"Me, too," says Jonathan. "I'm exhausted. Good night."

We all wave each other off, then the couple leaves for their bedroom.

As much as I always wanted to be with Abraham, he has never seen me without my wig or makeup. I'm not ready to show him. We can not sleep in the same space, but there's hardly any as it is. I try my best to think of an excuse to sleep on the recliner, or in my car.

The sound of Abraham's voice snaps me out of my concentration. "You should take a shower." I see that he's setting up the cot. "You don't have a single change of clothes?"

"Um, no. I don't."

"That's okay. You can borrow one of my shirts tonight. I'm still looking for work, but I have a good amount in savings. We'll work something out. I can get you an outfit or two."

He hands me a plain black T-shirt to wear.

"Thank you so much, Abe. I…"

He's looking at me so sweetly. In the past, there was always somewhere he needed to be, or I needed to be. Along with the distractions, there were other girls, and a lingering mystique. He's not lunging at me, hitting me, or forcing me to address him formally. He's tender, and he communicates. He was a nice break from the life I had. Now, there's nowhere else I need to be, and no more need to compete for his affection. He is unquestionably mine. The thought of that used to give me a lot of satisfaction. Now, it feels like a burden.

I take a deep breath. "I still want to take things slow. When I come out, can you make sure all the lights are off? I'd feel pretty self-conscious otherwise."

"Sure. I can do that."

"Thank you, Abe."

I step into the bathroom with my bag and Abraham's shirt. I lock the door behind me. The image in the mirror is startling. It's much bigger than the rearview mirror I'm accustomed to. The addition of my bloody clothes to my fake attributes makes the image even more unsettling. No wonder the others were so concerned. Not too long ago, I felt beautiful in my brown skin. At this moment, I feel filthy. I can't wait to wash everything off.

    I undress, place my wig on the counter, and pick out a washcloth and towel. Carefully, I use my hands to rinse the blood off my wig in the sink. I let it air dry on a door hook. In the shower, I use some of Lindsay's lemongrass-scented body wash. It's the nicest thing I ever rubbed on my body. I even put some in my hair. As I clean myself up, I use the detachable shower head to simultaneously rinse the makeup and blood off the tub floor and walls. I can't leave a single trace behind.

    When I finally get out and dry off, I put on Abraham's shirt. It barely covers my crotch, and it's surreal to see a piece of him on my white skin. I pick out a floral bonnet to tuck my blonde hair in. Once I finish that task, I put my mostly dry wig in my large bag, fold my clothes, and put my used panties back on. When I step out of the bathroom, it is very dark.

    "Go ahead and leave your bloody clothes on the counter in there." I can't see Abraham, but his tired voice is very clear. "We'll deal with them tomorrow. It's late."

    I feel my way around to the cot, and get under the covers. The pillow and blanket are thicker and warmer than what I'm used to. As soon as I get into a comfortable position, Abraham holds onto me from behind. My body tenses up immediately.

    "I just want to hold you. I'm not trying anything."

    "Okay."

    He pauses. "You smell good."

    "Thank you."

    There's a pause.

    "Feel a little bit better? You seem uncomfortable. Is this okay?"

    "Sorry. I… I'm fine, Abe. I'm just tired."

    "I understand." He gently kisses my neck.

My initial tension melts away. I'm not sure why my body responded like that in the first place. I turn, so that he's able to reach my lips. He kisses me softly, then deeply- filling me with sensations I'm not used to. I let him guide me onto my back. I don't think he's aware of the smile slowly forming on my face.

"I thought you weren't going to try anything."

"Do you want me to stop?"

I think about it for only a few seconds. "No."

26

"Educational milestones are deceptive to women, because they distract us from what we're meant to achieve."

I wake up abruptly and in a panic. The bright sunlight is seeping through the closed blinds. I have no idea how early or late in the morning it is, but I think I'm the only one who is awake. The bonnet is still in place. I grab Abraham's shirt and my panties from off the floor, and very cautiously put them on. I don't want to wake him- or anyone else- up. I get out of the covers, then snatch my purse as I tiptoe my way to the bathroom. I intend to put my bloody clothes back on, as well as my makeup and wig. The moment I open up the bathroom door, I hear Abraham's cracked voice.

"Morning, Gertie."

I look behind me to see Abraham stretching with his eyes closed. There's no telling how much he saw, but I can't risk him seeing more. I close the door behind me, then throw my wig and blood-stained clothes on. I'm about to apply my makeup, but before I have a chance to get started, there's a knock on the door.

"Dinah?"

It's Lindsay. "I forgot to tell you last night. Please don't put those clothes back on. Throw them out. You can borrow my stuff. Let me in real quick."

"I'm kinda naked right now."

"I'm sure we have the same parts."

"Doesn't matter."

"Fine. Open the door a crack, so I can throw the clothes in."

I do as suggested, making sure my face isn't seen. Then, I close and lock the door.

"Thank you, Lindsay. I'll hurry up."

The outfit consisted of panties, a long-sleeved shirt, and a long skirt. That's not what she normally wears. I'm touched by the sentiment. She didn't just grab random clothes. She picked out an outfit specifically for me. She sees me, and wants me to be comfortable. If that's her fulfilling a role, then what would be mine? Just to be comfortable?

After putting on the clothes and my makeup, I step out of the bathroom to see the trio back at the dining room table. Everyone else is dressed and eating cereal. The blinds are open, and the cot is already put away. Abraham's face lights up at the sight of me.

"Hi, Gertie."

"Hi, Abe."

I see Lindsay, and even crotchety Jonathan smiling at our interaction. I sit down with my phone handy. Finally, I take the time to look at it. There are dozens of notifications.

"The Discomfort had a busy night online."

Lindsay's eyes light up. "What are people saying?"

I scroll through the notifications. "I see that I'm going to have to block some people. There are spammy, mean messages by anonymous accounts. Lots of follows and comments. I'm trying to understand it all. Give me a moment here."

I scan through posts that we're tagged in. People are quickly gathering the facts of the night. Simple Watch members are saying they last saw David with a young woman. Of course, no one knew it was me. No one saw Jaxtyn at the Gate that night. They can't explain how his knife ended up on the scene. Some are accusing those Simple Watch members of making things up, and even covering up for Jaxtyn. All of the reasonable doubt is on my side. Other commenters are saying proof of a young woman's belongings were seen at the Clark residence. David, Quinn and Jaxytn were the only ones to know about me. Two of them can't talk, while one will probably be encouraged to not say anything at all.

Evans still brags about a consistently low crime rate, and Simples don't see themselves as violent. So, I can count on investigators glossing over most of the evidence. Any proof of a mysterious, young woman at the Gate and in the Clark home will be brushed off as rumors. Everything else will become propaganda. I have no intention of sharing any of this with the rest of The Discomfort, either. They're likely to pick apart details and dig deeper on any information I give them, so it's safer for me to play dumb.

"Hmm… There's a lot to unpack. Maybe I'm still waking up."

"Should we check the news?" Jonathan asks.

All of us nod in agreement. I'm not expecting the media to reveal more than the general public is, so I'm not worried. Jonathan uses his phone to connect one of his apps to the TV. A video pops up on the big screen. In it, a female news anchor says:

"President Evans is weighing in on the events. We will now go to the president's live morning press conference."

The video cuts to Evans standing at the presidential podium.

"People are using this incident to smear my leadership, and the morality of Simplicity. It does not reflect us one bit, but it does expose corrupt individuals hiding within our community. They need to be held accountable. Real Simples focus on marriage, family, and serving one another. We are a peaceful people. Quinn Clark and David Ferguson lived peaceful lives until they were brutally slain. Moreover, Mr. Ferguson's legacy is being tarnished with a vicious lie involving a child. There is no such kidnapped youth in the database, and no amount of government funds going into child laundering. I established Simplicity as a way to bring people together. Unfortunately, some want conflict. Discomfort. They want you to believe that some Americans are fed up, scared and ignored. In this country, we are capable of being whatever we want to be. If you want to be oppressed, then you've made your choice. It has nothing to do with the rest of us... who choose to live fruitful, honest, happy lives. Do not bow down to such blatant manipulation."

Jonathan disconnects the app from his phone. "I can't listen to any more of that."

Part of me is relieved by how predictable Evans is. I'm confident that no one will ever connect enough of the dots to find me. The other- much larger- part of me is disheartened. The block-in was filmed live. Everyone there was real, and had a lot to share. We inspired change. Instead of the event being seen as an opportunity to talk about why, Evans dismisses the whole thing as mischief. Simples will take his side, seeing and hearing what he wants them to. Nothing we do or say will ever matter- only his perception will.

As horrible as being a Simple was, the rules are clear. Everyone has a role, and certain outcomes are expected. I risked a lot to escape all of that, but I didn't bring anyone with me. I'm not trying to force all Simples to change. I wanted out for myself. Abraham, Lindsay and Jonathan want to change the whole system for everyone- despite some Blended people using their own voices in support of it. Rather than be open-minded to a difference in opinion- a right The Discomfort claims to support, those people are condemned. Maybe that's the downside to not having to perform. The lack of clarity... Simplicity... indeed leads to chaos.

When I first came to the Lowlands, there was so much vibrancy. I never saw so much joy and colors, and never felt more independent. Instead of recognizing it as a utopia, the people here complain. Nothing is enough. The Blended should be more furious with their parents than the government. The law is clear, but interracial couples continue to make the choice to be together and have kids anyway. They put themselves in harm's way, then claim their rights are being denied. I've tried to see the world through their eyes, but I just can't. I love the idea of women being able to make their own decisions. We should be more than wombs, cooks and washer machines, but I believe positive change can only be found within the system- not outside of it.

The whole block-in protest thing was a big waste of time. We just pissed people off, and there has been no game plan since then. I've been doing all of the work. People know about us, because of *me*. This isn't even my fight, and the other members never approved of anything I did... for *them*! I don't deserve insults and death threats. I don't need to live with so much uneasiness. I want better for myself.

This reminds me of something my mom warned me about as I was finishing high school. I heard rumors about non-Simple girls getting graduation ceremonies. I really wanted to have one, too.

She said something on the lines of, "Educational milestones are deceptive to women, because they distract us from what we're meant to achieve. It's a dizzying, deep rabbit hole. I heard Evans say, 'Desire for knowledge can never be satisfied, because the world contains too much information.' Simplicity isn't a hole. It's a path, and it leads directly to fulfillment."

Venturing outside of my comfort zone has burdened me. Wanting to be celebrated has distracted me. I choose to be fulfilled. In order for that to happen, I can not stay here.

27

"Friend of Gertrude's?"

    Breakfast was quite the experience. I didn't have to help with anything. There was no fancy decor or overabundance of food. I just ate a bowl of cereal that was served to me, and I didn't have to wait for the men to finish eating first. We were all eating together. Afterward, everyone put their own bowls and spoons in the sink. No one wiped down the table or counters. Lindsay and Jonathan actually washed the dishes together.
    Once the dishes were done, Jonathan and Abraham went out to look for work. Lindsay already found a job working in a stockroom for a clothing store, so she left for that. Before leaving for her shift, however, she gave me her copy of the front door key- in case of an emergency. She's very thorough and considerate. With the apartment finally empty, I head to the nearest drugstore to get a backpack, and a box of dark brunette hair dye. Once purchased, I head back to the apartment.
    While waiting on my hair to process, I raid the kitchen cabinets for non-perishable snacks. I put some of what I find in my new backpack. Then, I look through Lindsay's things in the

bathroom. I'm especially fond of her body wash, so I pack that, too. I also grab some of her clothes, combs and undergarments. She has such a great sense of style.

I take one last shower to rinse out my hair and foundation, then put the clothes back on that Lindsay had picked out. I look at myself in the mirror. My beige skin is a liberating sight. My dark hair... I love what I see, but I don't know who I'm looking at. I was never Dinah, and Gertrude is dead. This is my chance to be someone new- someone I actually want to be.

I throw my wig and leftover foundation in a plastic grocery bag, tie it, then shove it down into the kitchen trash can. I leave the extra key and my burner phone on the dining room table, then head towards the door. I'm ready for my new adventure. Before I get to the doorknob, however, it's already turning. The door opens. It's Abraham.

He's staring at me. I just stare right back. He takes his time walking in, his eyes never moving from mine until he turns around to close the door. Even though his body language is calm, I can tell he's very nervous. I am, too.

He brings his gaze back to me. "Friend of Gertrude's?"

I can't bring myself to speak, much less move the rest of my body. I have no idea how to get myself out of this situation. Gradually, Abraham's expression moves from worried to defeated. His voice remains the same.

"Were you ever going to tell me? What is this?"

My body still doesn't want to move, but I can't leave him without any sort of answer. I have to force the words out of me. "I'm leaving."

He nods, then looks down at the floor. He speaks under his breath. "I'm a fucking idiot."

"You're not an idiot, Abe."

He looks back up at me, with as much indifference as the day we met. "Where's Barbara?"

"I don't know."

"Your ex knew. You said you lost his number, but maybe you didn't want us to call him. He would have told us the truth about you, so you let her disappear."

"I didn't *let* her disappear. I didn't have anything to do with that."

He grunts. "So random… You coming across David's dead body like that. Unknown source. Did he know about you, too? Did Abril?"

"You are being way out of line."

I don't have to put up with this. I can push my way through, and never deal with him again. I know he won't bother chasing me, or trying to look for me later. I'm not even worried about him hurting me. Something I don't understand, however, is keeping my feet firm on the floor.

"*I'm* out of line!? Who the fuck are you!?"

I realize how tense my body is, so I do my best to relax it. I slowly breathe in and out. As I do, my eyes become watery. I stay focused on Abraham, so that he can see. As upset as I know he is, I want him to stay soft with me.

"I'm like you. I also pretend, so that I can survive."

He shakes his head. "I didn't lie."

"Not to me, but you planned on lying to everyone else. You bought skin bleaching cream."

"That *you* sold to me. While we're on the subject, are you still selling that shit?"

"Of course not. I told you I stopped."

Abraham sighs. He then sees my burner phone on the table.

I say, "I'm already signed in. You can change the password. I don't care. The Discomfort has over 900 followers. They're all yours."

He just looks at me. My couple of tears are doing nothing for him. I wipe them away. The silence is extremely uncomfortable, so I keep talking.

"I've built up quite a following. A lot of people are inspired."

"You inspired them with a lie. That was just a costume to you."

"Don't trivialize my experience! You have no idea what I've been through. I'm more myself than I've ever been. Through that skin, I felt beautiful, smart and accepted. I learned that I can make a difference in people's lives."

He scoffs. "Meanwhile, I walk around with the same skin tone, and I can be arrested. That is the best-case scenario. More than likely, I'd never be seen again. I keep a low profile, because that is safe. Thanks to you, strangers know me as an influencer's boyfriend. They know my face. This face… is not seen as a true American, or even human. I want that to change, and not just for me. The Discomfort isn't some vanity project. Fuck the follower count. And you… You were peddling skin bleach to black and brown people. Remember that? They can't feel beautiful and accepted in their skin? Was that your way of making a difference?"

"Don't be an asshole. You bought from me regularly. You wanted to pass as white."

"I wanted to be with my mother. I'm thankful my parents are reconciling, and I'm connecting with my father better than I ever have. I'm grateful, but I want more. I want to live in a world that allows us to be in each other's lives… as ourselves. It wasn't the whiteness I wanted. It was the privilege of acceptance and choice."

I roll my eyes. "I've never had any privileges. I didn't get to choose anything, and I was only accepted when I met other people's high expectations. My job was to be a wife and mother. That's it. But my husband hurt me, and the baby growing inside of me was taken away. Everyone else can chose, but I can't. So there's no use in feeling anything, or being attached to anything. The only constant I've ever had is fear. I've lived in fear my whole entire life, so you don't know what the hell you're talking about!"

Abraham's face doesn't change. "Okay. So fight for that. We're fighting against Simples as the Blended. You could recruit and inspire other Simple women to fight for equality. There were some at the block-in, so we already know allies exist. We could join forces, weaken Simplicity, and end Evans' presidency."

I'm speechless. All of that sounds dangerous and impossible. Besides, I can't reintroduce myself as a white-coded girl within the group. I'd never hear the end of it from the other members, and people on social media. The Simples would plot against me specifically, and probably want to investigate what happened to David and Quinn. No one would ever trust me. I would have so much to prove. I'm tired of proving myself. I just want to be.

Abraham chuckles. "Thought so."

"Huh?"

"Shit is getting too real, isn't it? Must be nice to be able to walk away."

"Don't try to guilt trip me. That's not fair! I'm as much of a victim of the system as you are! I just don't make it my whole identity. I choose to rise above that."

Abraham pauses before responding. "Wow."

"I mean, look at Twos. They move about freely. I know for a fact that Simples think very highly of them. I just don't understand. You guys are so quick to call them traitors, instead of opting for the freedom they have. You can live stress-free… harmoniously with the Simples, but you choose not to. I mean, even though that hashtag exposed a lot of them, we didn't hear about mass arrests."

"Doesn't mean it didn't happen."

"Look… I'm not going to fight with you."

For some reason, that makes Abraham smile. "Just go. Lindsay and Jonathan won't be back for a while. One is at work, while the other one is hustling to look for work. That's actually why I came back. I wanted to… spend some time with you."

I'm not sure how to respond. Honestly, I don't want to process anything. None of this makes me feel very good about myself. I am a good person, though. Abraham, understandably, enchanted me right away. He was unlike anyone I ever knew. I saw myself spending the rest of my life with him. Looking back, I saw him as an escape. Actually, Dinah did. I'm not Dinah, though. My path is different.

"Please, Abe. Take over the account. Do whatever you want."

I move around him to leave. He interjects. "People will ask about you."

"Tell them… I guess… something happened to me."

He grabs my arm. I'm startled, as I'm reminded of David grabbing me by the wrist.

"You fucking bitch. 'Take over the account.' You didn't just create an account. You put your face and name all over it. If something happens to you, it will be seen as a crack in the movement. People will panic, and go back into hiding. We're just barely beginning to mobilize. The Comfort law is gone, but something worse is coming. We still haven't found Abril or Barbara. No leads. None of that bothers you?"

I'm so exhausted by this whole thing. "I tried, Abraham."

He lets go of me. "Go fuck yourself."

I finally build the urge to leave, then I slam the door. I feel as if I've been let go from a cage. The sunshine and fresh air energize me instantly. When I get inside of my car, I take a big sigh of relief before starting up the engine. This time, I'm not heading back up the hill. I want to go beyond downtown and find

192

something new. The possibilities are endless and exciting. I paid my debts, and I belong to no one. I smile at myself in the rearview mirror, and tell myself that everything is finally going to be okay.

***

I want to chase after her, but I can't. I want to yell at her out the window, but I can't. I'd bring too much attention to myself. She knows that. I can't believe this is happening. I can't really be that mad at her, either. This is my fault. I'm the dumbass who trusted her, and fell for her. I can break the phone, though.

I rush over to the table. I'm more than ready to destroy the phone somehow, but the post-it note throws me off. I take a closer look at the password she left me:

4Abe&Oak

"Oak" probably has to do with someone else she conned. Poor guy. I take the phone, and go straight to the app. Dinah, Gertie… whoever she is… She's already signed in. I go under Account Settings, and replace her contact phone number with my email address. Then, I edit the password:

4B&AnotG

Saved. *Now*, I can fuck the phone up.

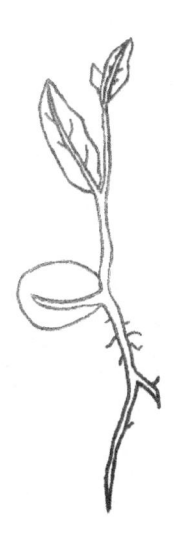

The story will continue through Abraham's perspective in 2024.
If you enjoyed COMFORT FOR COMMUNITY, please leave an honest review and tell a friend!

Instagram: instagram.com/heatherosoy_writes
Facebook: facebook.com/heatherosoywrites

Made in United States
Orlando, FL
01 December 2023